"I have to kiss you again..."

Irish's voice was thick and husky with emotion, and he pulled her close. "I've been begging myself not to . . . ."

"But I want you to." A sigh escaped Calico's lips as her soft breasts thrust against his chest. His mouth closed over hers, a glorious plundering.

She swayed against him, inviting him, aching for him, urging him. She was vibrantly alive, the way she felt when a storm swooped down the mountain. Only now the storm was within her, a raging tempest of desire. . . .

Dear Reader,

We at Harlequin are extremely proud to introduce our new series, **HARLEQUIN TEMPTATION**. Romance publishing today is exciting, expanding and innovative. We have responded to the ever-changing demands of you, the reader, by creating this new, more sensuous series. Between the covers of each **HARLEQUIN TEMPTATION** you will find an irresistible story to stimulate your imagination and warm your heart.

Styles in romance change, and these highly sensuous stories may not be to every reader's taste. But Harlequin continues its commitment to satisfy all your romance-reading needs with books of the highest quality. Our sincerest wish is that **HARLEQUIN TEMPTATION** will bring you many hours of pleasurable reading.

THE EDITORS

U.S.
HARLEQUIN TEMPTATION
2504 WEST SOUTHERN AVE.
TEMPE, ARIZONA
85282

CAN.
HARLEQUIN TEMPTATION
P.O. BOX 2800
POSTAL STATION "A"
WILLOWDALE, ONTARIO
M2N 5T5

Cast a Golden Shadow

JACKIE WEGER

Harlequin Books

TORONTO • NEW YORK • LONDON
AMSTERDAM • PARIS • SYDNEY • HAMBURG
STOCKHOLM • ATHENS • TOKYO • MILAN

Published April 1984

ISBN 0-373-25107-6

Printed in Canada

1

CALICO HAD NO IDEA how long she had dozed; not that it mattered much, for the storm that held her house-bound still raged over Talking Rock Mountain. As if to court her displeasure even more, a jagged rod of lightning flared with brilliance, sending a beam of light shooting into the cabin. Thunder following it echoed along sharp-edged rocks and gullies, causing her to feel a faintly annoying resurgence of energy. For a reason she couldn't fathom, storms affected her, spawning a formless wanting, a restlessness that lodged in the very core of her being. She loathed the feeling and the storm that forced her indoors so that she couldn't work off this throbbing energy.

Moving from the sofa, she added a log to the dying fire, then puttered around the cabin adjusting lamps to chase away gray shadows. When grampa died she would bring in electricity and install a bathroom. It was awful to think of it that way, and she didn't wish him dead, for she loved him, but he did want a same-ness about him. He never complained about changes in the world like the rest of the old-timers in Lumpkin County simply because he kept his own world a haven. He kept the cabin the way he remembered it during all those years he had been away before she had been born as though it was a corner of a dream he couldn't give up.

Calico wanted change, but she understood his rea-sons and respected them. Nothing had been changed in the cabin and it was filled with the presence of her grandmother Lucy, of her mother, Ellen, like an added layer of life.

She slept in a feather bed made by her grand-mother, kept warm with quilts sewn by her mother, and when she stood at the great ironstone sinks pumping water she had a sense of belonging, for the two women who had come before her had done the same.

Calico never felt lonely in the cabin. A far-thinking ancestor had built the vast main room of forty-foot pine harvested from the slopes of the mountain. The roof was high, the ceiling beamed with great thick logs darkened now with age, and along each side of the main chamber, roomy bedrooms had been added so that when one approached from the foot of the mountain, there was a sense of oneness, of coming upon something solid and everlasting. It was home, and Calico wanted to raise her own children there—if she ever had any.

She moved to her desk and sat down, fingering gold-bearing rocks that showed promise, but paying little attention because the restlessness that was upon her destroyed her concentration. Now and then she sighed and glanced out the window, able to see nothing beyond a gray sheet of rain as it pelted and exploded against the panes.

She tilted her chin and bent her head, listening to the damp wind-driven air, and for an instant her face was devoid of composure, stark and vulnerable. And then something, some noise, unexpected...an out-of-place sound whipping beneath the soughing of the wind caught at her.

Her hand swept to her neck, clutching at her throat as if to ward off choking. Her first thought was of her grampa, eighty-two years old, careening about the mountain, hurt or lost in an old abandoned mine, but she deflected that thought the instant it came into her mind. She knew exactly where he was. He was languishing in the great barn of a work shed behind the cabin finishing off a pint of homemade peach brandy, and by now no doubt, oblivious to the storm.

The broody hen that had made her nest in the old horsehair sofa on the front porch set up an alarming cackle. Calico shook her head in dismay. It seemed that everything on the mountain was going haywire. The old hen was out of tune with nature, trying to hatch a clutch of eggs in autumn instead of last spring. And nature herself seemed a little off-key, dumping this winter-frigid storm when all signs had suggested an Indian summer. The sound came again and she listened intently. It was faint but growing stronger and finally she recognized it for what it was; a dog barking, though the sound was eerily muffled by the rain. Dropping her hand to her lap with a relieved sigh, she looked through the window trying to see beyond the rain, but all she could see was her own reflection, softened by the glow of the kerosene lamps.

Her face had a certain cast, something indefinable, a substance that suggested secret knowledge. Perhaps it was the proud way she had of carrying herself, or that backwoods manner she had of looking directly at you. Whatever it was, it made you keep on staring. But there was no one about to stare at her now, so she rose to her feet and shrugged into an aged yellow slicker, so old and worn it had the feel of supple silk.

She emerged onto the porch to be sheltered from the storm that expressed the very essence of the wild North Georgia mountain on which she'd been born and lived her life. Her back was straight, her long legs clad in fitted cords that were tucked into her bout du nords, her thick auburn hair braided and held with a piece of string. All these things were one with the ragged mountain, but it was her eyes and her expression that made one suspect her depth, which was as hidden as the subterranean tunnels that cut through the mountain's bowels.

Her eyes were gray, almost silvery and deep set, so that they enhanced cheekbones planed into a strong angle that gave off an accurate impression of self-willed self-sufficiency and self-reliance. The shape of her mouth was at once stubborn and sensuous, and after her eyes, her most noticeable feature. Those who knew her best were caught up in her vitality, and no one ever stopped to notice whether she was beautiful or not. Calico suspected not. No one had ever said. Not in her entire thirty years. And she felt alien from her people in some way. Different from her grandfather, Christian and her cousins, Jebediah and Winnie, themselves nearly as old as grampa.

The barking rose like a panic, snapping off her reflections, and then the pup leaped from the curtain of rain into the yard, wailing like a banshee. All six or seven wringing wet pounds of him, popping up and down like a wind-up toy one bought at carnivals. Tags clinked and dangled from his collar, so that Calico surmised he wasn't the spawn of wild dogs roaming the mountains. Jumped out of a tourist's car most likely, she thought.

"Shoo! Shoo!" she shouted, but at the sound of her voice the dog just became more worked up than ever. It ran up the porch steps, stirring up the old hen, and then down again, racing on its short legs toward the swollen river and back to bound around her once more.

Calico shook her head. She hated to shoot dogs. She hated *to have* to shoot even the wild, dangerous ones that ran in packs, and didn't unless they became a real nuisance. She wasn't about to go chasing after this one, but if it settled down, she'd put it in the shed until she could see about finding its owner.

The pup dashed down the hummock to the river

again. Her gaze followed him and she noticed the tree, its gargantuan root span dragging in shallow water like a beached whale. The dog leaped into the torrent and lost himself in the branches of the downed tree.

He's a goner, she thought, having no sympathy for an animal that should have its instincts about it. Not even the beavers that lived on the river had remained in their lodges during this storm. They sensed the coming of raging flood waters, and it was a good thing, too. If that tree had come down above the sluice, the beaver lodge was gone now. The top of the tree lay submerged in the roiling waters, the current dragging it so that its roots cut a groove on the river-bed. Calico mapped the path in her mind. Down to bedrock, she thought, and marked it mentally as a spot to set up her dredges and gold-panning equipment.

Suddenly the dog reappeared, scudding along the length of the trunk. Calico's jaw gaped in surprise. It was too curious a behavior to ignore. She ventured down the hummock to the river's edge, using her hand to protect her eyes from the driving rain.

The dog was now lost to her view among the pine boughs submerged in the water, but she heard it whining piteously. Then she gasped. A human foot, bare, swayed in the churning waters. Now she saw a leg, two legs, a torso twisted against branch stubble that jutted skyward.

Skirting the roots, she waded into the river and climbed upon the trunk, moving across old scars in the bark, where beavers had chewed and bears had sharpened their claws, to the dark-haired man tangled in the branches.

It took her some minutes to free the body, and as she struggled with it, the tree began to move, slowly, shudderingly, dragging the riverbed, the tons of roots marking a trough, shoving boulders and red clay be-

fore them like a giant earth mover. She grabbed the
man's shirt, flailing into the river, pulling him behind
her as she lurched her way to shore.

In the water he seemed weightless; out of it, he was
heavy and limp, like a soggy sack of wet flour. She
laid him out in the mud, stretching out beside him for
a moment to catch her breath while the rain shot out
of the sky, stinging and cold. The man looked dead.
She shivered, putting her hand over his heart and
feeling it beating, not strong, but beating. She turned
him on his stomach, pumping his arms, watching to
see if he spit up any water. It was then she saw the
gash on the back of his head. She turned him over,
grabbed his shoulders and shook him mightily.

"Can you hear me? Were you alone?" she screamed
above the roar of the wind, and knew it was no use.
His head flopped forward, limp, unconscious. She
wondered if there was a woman, perhaps even children, floating, drowning somewhere in the river and
if that was so, knew too, that there was nothing she
could do. She sat back on her heels to think while
water ran from her boots. His pockets! She searched
them, finding only mud and gravel. No wallet, no
keys, not even a dime.

She was soaked to the skin and the cold penetrated
to bone. But this stranger was not going to wake up
and walk himself up the hill to the cabin. She left him
lying there, with his pup hanging about and went to
get her grandfather, praying silently that he wasn't
yet too drunk to be of use. She had long ago grown
used to grampa's peculiarities. He lived in the past,
and was obstinately against change that could have
provided them with electricity, telephone, and inside
plumbing. He was in many ways a sad old man, and
she didn't push him, not often, anyway.

She shoved open the wooden door of the work shed
and peered inside, spying him out. A kerosene lantern

hung from a beam, casting a soft golden glow among old hoes, rakes, dredges and split logs drying for the cookstove. She spied his bushy gray head tilted back against the old stump on which they chopped wood.

"Grampa! I need your help. I've just found a man, a stranger, in the river. He's hurt and I need help to get him up to the house."

Christian moaned slightly and her heart sank. He was drunk... far drunker than she'd seen him in a long while. She moved closer.

"Grampa?"

"I've been calling you," he said. His voice, always gritty and hoarse, sounded weak. Calico felt a thread of alarm.

"Grampa! Are you sick?" She reached his side, and knelt down. One of his legs was bent at a funny angle and tucked beneath the other. "Did you fall?"

His eyes were squeezed closed in pain and all thoughts of the stranger, all the questions that had risen in her mind, faded. "Cut my blamed toes off chopping wood," he whispered through his pain. "Axe slipped. Never even felt the hurt for a full five minutes."

Calico swallowed and looked again at his legs, and then pulled the hidden one out to where she could see it clearly. He had managed to get his boot off and make a tourniquet with his belt. She felt a prick of nausea sweep into her throat. "I'll have to go for help," she told him.

He shook his shaggy head, his mouth working to force sound between his lips. "I'll bleed to death before you get back. You'll have to sear it first."

"Sear it?" she said, barely audible, knowing what he meant, not liking it and swallowing the bile rising in her throat. "I can't."

His lids flew open, revealing translucent blue eyes, stark with pain. "Either do it, or go on up to the cabin and let me die in peace." He wasn't making an attempt at dramatics, just resigning himself to a situation over which he had no control.

Knowing more talk was useless, Calico slipped her arm beneath her grandfather's and half carried, half dragged him into the cabin.

The next hour went by in a blur that would remain forever a blur in her memory. She worked by feel, fought nausea, not thinking about what she was doing or what her grandfather might be feeling.

The odor of burnt flesh hung in the air as she stumbled from his room in somber stupefaction, trembling with the enormity of what she had just done. She collapsed into a chair and rested her head on folded arms, sinking into a stupor. At the back of her mind something nagged just out of reach. She tried hard to remember, raising her eyes to the kerosene lamp above the oaken table, as if its golden glow could penetrate into her brain and illuminate the dark recess that hid the thought. There came a soulful, mournful howl that made her jerk upright. The stranger!

She had left him lying on the riverbank. A furious wave of guilt rushed over her. He was probably dead for sure by now, of exposure, pneumonia, or perhaps the rain beating into his face had drowned him as the river had not. She hurried outside, panic thudding against her ribs. The air was full of river spray and the roar of rushing water. The huge pine was gone, taken downriver and round the mountain.

The awful howling rose, magnified as all sounds whirled together. She reached the man just as the rising angry current was snatching at his limp body. Please let him be alive, she prayed. Not to God, because she no longer trusted him to do anything straightforward, but to the spirits she believed inhabited the mountain. She locked her arms about his chest and began to drag him uphill. He was heavy, long and unwieldy, and every backward footstep, every inch gained, was sheer torture.

She negotiated the old wooden steps one at a time, dragging her burden, gasping for breath and not daring to let up until she had him on the floor in front of the fireplace. The pup slipped past her as she went back to close the door. There was nothing more distasteful to her than the smell of wet dog, but he curled up by the fire and she let him be.

She knelt on the floor beside the man, staring fixedly at his face. It was scratched, blue from cold, and slack, giving her no hint of what he was like, what his thoughts might be or the nature of his character. But she had pulled him from the river, from certain death, and in a way, that made him belong to her. A feeling of possessiveness began to build in her.

Above all things she wanted to be married, to have children, to have a husband, *to love*. These things had been denied her because of a single dreadful event in her past, a secret she guarded with her every waking moment. In Appalachia men had but one prerequisite for their brides, and in the intimacy of a marriage bed she would be found out. So she pretended to all that she wanted nothing to do with men, that marriage didn't appeal to her.

Gazing now at the stranger with a passion she seldom revealed, she let her mind and body wander ahead recklessly. She wished he would wake up and speak, willing him to open his eyes. When he didn't, she sat back to remove her boots, then set about doing what she could to keep him alive, for alive he still was. She was wet and muddy and feeling bruised herself, yet a sudden surge of energy enveloped her. She knew she had to work fast. Her grandfather needed a doctor and she'd have to leave them both while she went for help.

She built up the fire until it was blazing. She stirred
banked embers in the wood stove and set a quilt and
towel to warming. Then she bathed and bandaged the
stranger's head, taking note of his fine thick hair as
she washed the mud from his face and neck. He had
hawklike irregular features that she tried to visualize
animated, and her curiosity about him rose. With
scissors she cut away his shirt, finding a badly bruised
chest covered with a mat of curling black hair. She
talked to him all the while, hoping that the sound of
her voice would bring him around.

She took a deep breath and began cutting away his
pants, seeing that each part of him fit perfectly with
the next. She hesitated over his undershorts, but only
for an instant and cut them away too. She tried not to
look *there*, but couldn't help herself. Her face flamed.
Even lying there on the floor before the fire, unconscious, unaware of his surroundings, he was impres-
sive. She felt herself grow warm from the study of his
body, and the warming flicked at her nerves with un-
explainable need. Goose bumps erupted along his
arms and legs, and feeling a thrust of shame, she hurriedly wrapped him into the warm quilt, put a pillow
beneath his head and made herself ready to go down
the mountain to get Doc Willis. But as she changed
into dry clothes, her curiosity remained so high-
pitched she found herself at his side every few minutes.

She begged herself not to, but she couldn't resist
touching him, watching her hand move like some
alien appendage over which she had no control, sliding through silky, curling dark hair. She bent close,
intrigued with the spicy male scent that lingered on
his finely textured skin.

"Hallooo! Anybody home?"

Calico snatched her hand from the man, slapping it
against her own breasts, gasping with a sense of

shame as the blood stopped moving in her veins. Quickly she rose to her feet and moved away from him toward the front of the cabin.

At the door she found herself facing a dripping Gabe Tarrant, the oldest son of her best friend, Jobeth. At fourteen he was as tall and powerfully built as his father, Judalon, but he had his mother's fair coloring and an angelic face. Calico liked him and didn't hold it against him that he had sprung from the loins of a man she hated. Though at this moment she needed help and would've welcomed the devil himself. 'Gabe!' she exclaimed. "What're you doing out of school and wandering around in this weather?'' She grabbed his wrists, pulling him into the house.

His blue eyes opened wide with shock at her wild appearance, and grew wider still as his gaze landed on the quilt-clad man lying on the hearth. "Gawd! Did you kill him? Was he after your gold? Gawd! Wait until Lumpkin County hears about this!''

"Gabe. Be quiet! I pulled him from the river. I didn't hear the truck come up. Who's with you?'' she asked, needing to get her thoughts in some practical order.

Reluctantly Gabe gave her his attention. "Ma. We stopped at the old trestle bridge. River's pushed a tree up against it. Ma was afraid to drive across it, it was shaking so bad. She wants to know if you've seen pa.'' He looked down at his feet, embarrassed. "He ain't been home all night and me and ma, we're out looking for him.'' There was a resentment in his voice, which he swallowed almost at once.

"I haven't seen him,'' she said. And she'd better not. Tarrant knew better than to come on Talking Rock. "Listen, Gabe, Grandpa's had an accident, and—'' she waved her hand casually at the quilt "—this man needs doctoring, too. I want you to go back down the mountain. Tell your mother to drive like lightning for Doc Willis and send him up here, and hurry." She pushed him out the door, giving him no time for more questions. "Run!" she called after him as he loped off, splashing through the mud, his head sunk down in his coat against the autumn storm.

After he disappeared around the bend in the lane, Calico turned back into the cabin and went into her room to prepare her bed for the stranger, never for a single instant entertaining the thought that Doc Willis might send him to the hospital.

2

CALICO HAD A GREAT SENSE OF WORTH about herself as a modern-day placer miner, but none whatsoever about herself as a woman, modern or otherwise. Her sexual growth had been stunted years before and that had left its mark upon her. As she cared for the man lying at her feet, her sexuality began to bloom, bursting with blundering and uncommon speed to rail at the barrier of her reserve.

In the stringent manner in which she thought of herself she had only one allowable vanity: skin care. She prospected and mined gold from the surfaces of frozen rivers in icy winds that chapped, worked long sweat-drenched hours beneath hot summer suns that burned or guided tourists that swarmed into Dahlonega on gold hunts—and they always thought stumping through the forest to an inaccessible stream was necessary if they were to find that record lump of gold. It was rough hard work and she didn't want to look like a dried-up prune, so she bathed and pampered herself with extravagant oils and soaps scented with lavender and lilies. They were fragrances of the earth and made her feel clean, mysterious and sometimes exotic.

She yearned for one of those baths right now. She checked on her charges, and when she felt she could leave them she pulled the old-fashioned tub from behind the wood stove and began filling it with water from the stove's reservoir. She shampooed her hair and braided it wet while soaking in the tub, con-

stantly alert to every sound inside the cabin and
without. Her grandfather's breathing was tortured,
and the stranger's, though shallow, was even. Yet
when he emitted a low moan she went flying out of
the tub, dripping lily-scented water onto the floor as
she ran to him and knelt at his side. Turning down
the quilt, she took his hands into her own. His
fingers were long with tufts of dark hair at each
digit, the nails square, and his palms were free of
callouses. Competent hands, she thought, admiring
them, noting that his left hand was free of a marriage
ring.

His face was metamorphosing, taking on character,
losing its slackness. Suddenly the hands lying dormant in hers began to fold over her fingers with sur-
prising strength. Calico was electrified.

Irish McCaulley was coming awake. He knew it.
What he didn't know was if he was waking up dead
or just waking up. There was a horrible pain behind
his eyes, sharp darting pulses that kept him from
opening his eyes shooting from temple to temple. He
felt himself submerged in a barrage of sensations and
he sluggishly attempted to catalog them.

There was an evocative smell of woodsmoke, the
pungency of kerosene with which he was familiar,
and something else, a trace of flowers, and those he
couldn't identify. He was dry and warm. He hadn't
been—he dimly remembered the cold—and a cork-
screw of fear ripped into his gut. He didn't want to be
dead; he had too much work ahead of him, no matter
that his whole life seemed to be at a dead end. *Don't
think dead anything,* he warned himself.

He recognized the flowers now. Lilies, damn it! He
was dead. But the dead weren't supposed to feel pain,
and he was racked with it. He couldn't breathe, there
was a stricture of some sort in his chest, and his leg
hurt as though a hot poker had been jammed into it.

It seemed to take hours, but he forced his eyes open, unable to focus for several interminable seconds so that he was certain that if not dead, he was at least blinded. A vision began to take shape before him, and he discovered himself looking into the most remarkable gray eyes, magnificent quicksilver eyes, huge and somber in their shadowy hollows. A strange chill crept up his spine. His gaze dropped and he was seeing—unbelievably—the naked glistening body of a nymph, and he caught the uneven sound of her quickened breath. The nymph spoke in a soft melody. "Who are you? Was anyone with you?"

He decided he was alive but lost to the world of reality. He tried to nod and couldn't, the pain in his head too shocking, the tightness in his chest excruciating, leaving no room for air. He managed a garbled, "Sam."

When she saw his lips moving, Calico bent her head to them and the slight movement caused her bare breasts to touch his naked arm. She jerked back, burning with this new sense of intimacy, snatching up a corner of the quilt to cover her nakedness. "Another man, did you say?" Her voice was shaking.

Irish thought she sounded like a melodious treble. His Adam's apple flexed. "Dog," he sputtered, drawing out the syllable, but the effort was too much. The flaming auburn hair of the nymph began to spin, faster and faster like the ultracentrifuge in his laboratory, and the color went deeper until everything was black and the soft center of his brain was jumping all over his past. He tried to hold it still, to command it to stop, but there was Sister Antonio's face, distant and unreal, and he saw her hands thin and delicate, jutting from beneath starched white cuffs. She was twisting the gold wedding band that announced she was a virgin bride of Christ, and he was a little boy again. The shrinking hurt his head.

"Go into the kitchen now, Irish, stay with Sister Sophie until I call you."

He didn't want to remember this, he wanted it erased from his memory, but there it was indelibly, and he heard his answer. "But...but, it's open house today. People will be coming to look for children to adopt. If I'm in the kitchen, how will they get to see me?" His stomach was in knots. He had been waiting, planning, anxious for this day to arrive.

"They don't want grown children, they want babies," Sister Antonio told him. "You're seven years old, almost a man." She smiled down at him, ivory faced, ivory teeth, pale lips, an ivory blur wrapped in a black habit to give her substance. "Go into the kitchen like I told you."

He took a reluctant step backward. "But *Sister*," he protested desperately. "Allen got adopted and he was nine!"

The ivory blur flushed pink. "You can't be adopted, Irish. That's the end of it. Now go! And none of your foolish tantrums. Sister Sophie will give you milk and cookies."

He stumbled from the entrance foyer where he had stationed himself to be the first child seen. He looked neat, he knew he did. His cowlick was plastered down with Vitalis and his shirt didn't have a smudge on it. He had planned to pick himself some parents as much as they picked him. He didn't need food. He needed someone to love him. *Why wasn't he adoptable?* Was there something inside himself that he couldn't see? Did they whisper about him as they did of eight-year-old Effie, perfect in every way on the outside, but something so mixed up inside that she would always be just a sweet adorable baby?

You can't be adopted. He tried to expell the memory, lose himself in a painless vacuum, but the pain was real, febrile, and the thread of one patch of memory knotted inseparably with the next and there was Sister Antonio again, chastising him for standing at the wavy mirror at the end of the damp hall in the dormitory.

"Stop admiring yourself, Irish. Conceit is a sin."

"I'm not admiring myself, sister, I'm trying to see what's inside." And he had spent his life looking inside, but there was nothing defective, no tainted poisoned parts until he came to his soul. It was flat and fluttery like a dead leaf and it floated out of his reach. He lurched for it and there was the nymph again....

"Quit thrashing about!" Calico shouted, again and again. "You're hurt, you're only making it worse!" She threw herself across his chest, holding him down. Finally he lay quiet, tranquility overtaking his features.

She could see blood beginning to seep through the bandage on his head, but there was a sensation upon her now that left her dazed. As she raised herself up off his broad chest, her nipples grazed lightly the wiry hair on his chest. The feeling sent the most incredible warmth into her loins, a warmth that seemed to cling to her as she dressed. She couldn't make it go away. She wasn't sure she wanted it to. The dog began to yap, and the sound so startled her Calico caught her breath. Her first thought was that the strange man was dying, that the dog had sensed it and set up a howl. She left her grandfather's side, rushing into the main room only to find the pup squatting before the door. She let him out and followed him out onto the porch.

The storm had blown itself out, though the sky remained slate gray. She inhaled the freshly washed air, finding it cold, but not frigid. Perhaps they'd have an Indian summer after all. She hoped so. It was then she heard the motors grinding, inching up the lane that led into the yard. Several motors, not just Doc Willis's.

She should have expected it. Whenever there was

trouble, friends and family showed up to help. It was Appalachian courtesy. There was Doc Willis, Jobeth and Gabe, who had fetched the doctor, and cousin Winnie Bascomb, sitting up straight as a board next to her husband, Jebediah.

Winnie was as lean and thin as Jebediah was square and squat. She admitted to seventy-two years, her generation thinking it was ladylike to be ten years younger than their husbands. Calico suspected Winnie was far older, but she moved like a sprite in her freshly starched apron that she wore like a badge of honor. Jebediah was stern and taciturn and didn't go to church, which humiliated Winnie, who was always name dropping about God. She was sly and subtle about it most times, but if you listened to her long enough, you'd think He lived just around the corner from her house at the foot of the mountain. Calico loved her, but had never been able to talk with her, the generation gap being a span that neither could reach across. Besides that, Calico had stopped believing in an ethereal God, a transparent God, a God who left no shadow and deserted her when she had called out for him to save her from Judalon Tarrant. And Winnie didn't understand this about her either.

Jobeth was her own age, but that relationship, too, had been strained until Calico had got the knack of cordoning off that part of her brain that knew Judalon for what he was, keeping it separate, so that she could continue her friendship with his wife.

Abraham Willis was the first to reach her, as she stood upon the porch waiting. He was tall, his bones knitted together haphazardly, yet he was kind, with small hands as delicate as a city woman's. And gentle, too, she knew. He had set her arm when she broke it years ago.

"Thank you for coming so quickly," Calico greeted him.

He smiled, his bald brow wrinkling, as he led her into the house, the others close on their heels. "Professional courtesy, and glad to," he replied. "You know it was me your grampa was delivering that day his wife died, more than half a century ago, now, and don't remind me, but I owe the old man something for that. Let's go see him."

"Doc Willis," Calico whispered hesitantly. "Please don't mention anything about grampa's past and him being a doctor...it gets him all fired up and then he falls into depression." *Drinks himself into it,* she added mentally, *then holes up in some old mine or cave, leaving me to worry myself sick.*

"Of course I won't," Doc answered, patting her arm.

She led him into Christian's room as she told him what had happened. "Grampa's in a lot of pain, running a fever now and I think delirious. He's been calling for Grandmother Lucy...." Her voice trailed off.

"Don't worry about that. Trauma does that sometimes, plays tricks on our minds. I'll take care of the pain right away." He opened his bag, drawing out syringes, vials, gauze.

Jebediah reeled into the room, his face as gray as Christian's was white and bloodless. He had been a distant cousin to Lucy, who had been Christian's wife, and he was cousin to Calico, how much more distant she didn't know, but blood kin was blood kin. "What kind of an accident—" he began and then saw his old friend's foot. "Lord a mercy! Axe?"

"Yes, and I had to cauterize it," said Calico, her voice strained as she relived the memory of that awful moment. "Grampa made me."

Doc Willis stopped his examination of Christian and looked at her sharply. There were, he thought, signs that she was at the end of the tether. "This old

badger can get through the rest of his days without
his toes. You saved his life. Now, Jeb can help me in
here. You go on in the kitchen, get one of the ladies
to make you some tea. You look like you need it.''
When Calico just stood there, he raised his voice.
''Scat!''

She went.

Jobeth and Gabe were standing over the stranger in
front of the sofa. Calico advanced a step in their direction, changed her mind and moved toward Winnie
instead. Always the practial one, the old woman was
at the great ironstone sink, pumping water into a
kettle. She stopped and threw her arms about Calico.
''What's happened up here, child?'' she asked. ''You
took a man from the river and Christian's had an
accident?''Calico told her the events of the afternoon,
glossing over as much as she dared about the man
because she felt her face going warm each time she
mentioned him. And she still had the funny sensation
of warmth hovering about her thighs, so that she felt
the urge to sit.

As she listened, Winnie sensed Calico was holding
something back. She had always suspected there was
something wrong with the girl. Not wrong as in
sinned wrong, but that her aim in life had gone awry
somehow. She had tried over the years to delve into
this secretiveness that Calico projected but was no
nearer to understanding it now than she had been in
the past.

As Calico continued to explain the afternoon's
events, Winnie found her mind wandering. She didn't
like it that Calico wasn't married, that she was so alone.
Of course, she lived up here with her grampa, but that
was almost like living the life of a hermit, what with
Christian being so soured on life himself, and drinking
like he did. It wasn't fittin' for a young woman. And no
amenities. Now there was a sin.

Calico had enchantress eyes, and Winnie worried they were going to get her in trouble with the Lord one day. Those eyes could suck you in, make you plumb forget what you'd been saying. If she didn't know for a fact that Calico had been ejected from her mother's womb up on this very mountain, she'd swear by all the saints that the child had sprung from the bowels of the mountain, all by herself. Course she never said that aloud, else her quilting circle would think she'd gone rocker-crazy, but there was something queer about Talking Rock killing Calico's ma and pa, then spittin' Calico back. But Calico was Calico, and there was no getting around that. Determined she was, and stubborn, too.

"I've been talking to you, Winnie, and you haven't heard a single word!" said Calico, her expression puzzled.

"My mind's on this mess," Winnie said swiftly, re-pinning the silky white knot of hair at the back of her head. "Look at that floor, tracked with mud, and no telling what else. Soon's the teas's ready, I'll get to mopping. Your color's high. Best you sit until you've got something warm inside. Probably you ain't eat all day."

"I'm fine, really," Calico protested. She longed to join Jebeth and Gabe at the hearth, but she imagined that she couldn't walk over there casually enough for anyone not to discern what was in her mind. So she sat at the huge old oak table that Jebediah had built as a wedding gift to Christian and his bride and waited for tea.

"Where do you suppose the stranger came from?" Winnie asked.

Calico shrugged. "The mountain gave him up." In truth, that was the only thing that mattered to her.

Winnie gave her a sharp glance and sighed. Talking Rock had once been the sacred place of the Cherokees, a place of ritual, of myth, of occult ceremonies—all of it now covered with rhododendron slicks, cudzu and pine. It was no wonder Calico was the way she was. The wild mountain hadn't changed in a thousand years, but Winnie thought it was strange doings, the mountain repeating itself like it had. First it had given up Calico, and now this man.

Calico was becoming apprehensive. Abraham Willis and Jebediah had been with her grandfather a long, long time. If Doc Willis didn't get to the stranger soon, he might die. She was fearful that his breath might be leaving him any minute. She kept glancing surreptitiously at Gabe and Jobeth to see if their faces reflected any alarm. Not so far. Her tea sat before her on the table, untasted. Every time Winnie looked over at her she put her hand on the cup, as if she were just about to take a sip, but she couldn't. She couldn't swallow; it'd be impossible. She'd choke to death trying. When Jobeth began to move toward her, ponderously because she was in the advanced stage of her seventh pregnancy, Calico nearly leaped from her chair. But the only expression on Jobeth's wide freckled face was one of concern. Not concern for the man, or Christian, or, Calico soon discovered, for her. After Jobeth poured herself a cup of tea from the kettle kept warm on the stove, she lowered herself into a chair across from Calico.

"You sure you ain't seen Judalon up here anywhere?" she asked.

Calico stiffened. "No. I told Gabe I haven't."

Jobeth shook her head, as if she couldn't countenance the reply. "He's up here somewheres, I just know it. He's off looking for that old Spanish treasure and you know everyone says it's on Talking Rock."

"There's no Spanish treasure," said Calico. "It's just talk to draw tourists. Judalon will turn up when he gets tired and hungry. He wouldn't come up here anyway. He knows grampa doesn't like anyone poking around up here."

Jobeth sniffed. "He must not mind too much, he leased off a couple of acres, didn't he? To that realtor from down to Atlanta?"

"That was a long time ago, and grampa'd been drinking. Besides, we needed the money, then." This chitchat might be fine for Jobeth, but Calico couldn't keep her mind on it. She wondered what was taking Doc Willis so long with her grandfather. He could've sewn up twenty pairs of feet by now.

"You're looking kinda pale," Jobeth observed. "I ain't seen you so white since I told you I was going to marry Judalon." She feigned a small laugh. "I never have got over that—not in fifteen years. I thought you were in love with him, too. That worried me, y'know. If you wanted him, I knew I didn't have a chance." A sharp accusatory tone overrode the self-pity in Jobeth's voice. Calico's mouth went dry. She burned to know why Jobeth was slanting talk this way. There were so many conflicting emotions running wild inside her, it took a heartbeat for her to compose her reply.

"You're too hard on yourself, Jobeth. I said that too. I've never wanted Judalon. Stop talking like that."

"How come you ain't never married, then? A woman don't come on thirty without wanting a man. It ain't natural. Your sex is just waiting to explode up inside you—"

"Nothing is going to explode up inside me," Calico snapped indignantly, feeling this minute that Jobeth had never before uttered a truer statement. She was becoming annoyed, and showed it. The hollows in her cheeks were more pronounced, her eyes flashed warningly, but Jobeth ignored the signs and kept on, driven by something deep inside her.

"Answer me, then. I just want to know. Why haven't you ever married?" she demanded.

"I don't want to, and that's all the answer you're going to get out of me, Jobeth Tarrant." She was so agitated she accidentally took a sip of the cold tea and nearly gagged.

"Don't want to!" Jobeth exclaimed, careful not to sneer. "Scared to, you mean. Still a virgin, no doubt!"

"No—" The word just popped out, slipping between her lips before she had a chance to choke it back. A gasp of air floundered in her throat. She shrank in dismay, her cheeks angrily aflame, and thought she noticed a visage of coy triumph on Jobeth's wide face, but it was so suddenly replaced with a stricken look, she wasn't sure.

"Who—?" Jobeth pressed in an inaudible rasp, her face gone so pale her freckles appeared to leap and dance across her cheeks.

Calico's brain whirled. *The man you married. The man you said you were taking on because he wouldn't take no for an answer. The man you said you were marrying so all the girls in Lumpkin County would be safe.... But you were too late! Too late!* She took a deep breath, looking at Jobeth through a sweep of thick lashes. "It doesn't matter," she said grimly. But it did matter; it robbed her of being whole, it robbed her of her dreams.

Doc Willis and Jebediah emerged into the room just then, their expressions solemn. Winnie stopped mopping over by the front door, Gabe glanced up, Jobeth twisted around in the chair, Calico was riveted, unable to move, and the silence was so deep that for a moment she imagined she had the cabin to herself. Doc Willis's arm encircled Calico's shoulders.

"Don't look so worried. Old Doc Jones is going to be fine. I'm going to take him down to the hospital. He needs whole blood, and I'm going to have to take some skin off his skinny old flanks to make a cushion over his wound."

Somehow Calico managed to find her voice. "Grampa's going to be all right then?"

"Right as rain if he doesn't catch pneumonia," Doc assured her. "Now, let's check on your uninvited guest." He advanced on the quilt-clad figure, knelt beside him as Calico had done, and began inspecting the congealed gash on his head, the bruised broad chest with its mat of dark wiry hair, folding the quilt down farther and farther.

Calico felt Jobeth at her elbow, but she ignored her, submerging for the moment the anger she felt for her friend. The man was all-important to her. She didn't consider him to be uninvited. She believed in fate, believed that the spirits roaming Talking Rock had brought them together. Her single worry now was that he might be carried off the mountain and out of her reach. Doc Willis angled a look up to all the faces crowding around.

"Do you ladies mind...?" he asked with a trace of disgust. "This man is naked. We can preserve his modesty...."

"But I've already—" Calico began and stopped abruptly, turning scarlet.

Doc Willis shook his bald head. "I need some hot soapy water," he ordered gruffly, issuing the command to no one in particular. Winnie and Jobeth beat a hasty retreat to the kitchen. Calico refused to budge.

"What are you going to do to him?" she asked.

"Sew up his scalp, bind up his ribs—one's broken—have a look at the rest of him, when you—"

"He woke up once," she interjected anxiously, desperate that Doc Willis not find anything so wrong that the man would be whisked off down the mountain and out of her life.

"Find out who he is?"

"No, just that he's alone, except for his dog."

Leaning back on his haunches, the doctor studied Calico cryptically, analytically, for a moment, then took a thermometer out of his bag, shook it down and handed it to her. She accepted it, thinking he meant for her to assist him. He disabused her of that idea at once. "Put this under your tongue and go sit at the table," he ordered. "I'll get to you directly."

"But, nothing's wrong with me!" she protested panic-stricken that he might think her sick and unable to look after the stranger.

"Tell Winnie to bring me that soapy water," he said by way of answering her, and Calico, seeing the stubborn set of his jowls, had little choice but to retreat as had Jobeth and Winnie.

Five minutes later the thermometer was read and Winnie announced that Calico had no temperature. At that same moment a low groan issued from the area of the hearth. Calico leaped up, rushed across the room and knelt at Doc Willis's side. "What's the matter?"

"Back!" he ordered.

"Not until you tell me what you're doing to him!"

"By all the saints!" he growled. "You're worse than a mother with a newborn! I'm removing a thick splinter from his leg...."

"But, you're *hurting* him...."

Abraham Willis snorted with full-fledged disgust. Setting aside his tweezers, he reached into his black bag, took out a syringe, filled it from a tiny vial and held it in front of Calico's nose. "You see this, Calico Jones? There's enough stuff in this to knock you out for *two* days, and if you come near me or interrupt one more time...."

Appalled, Calico thrust out her chin, sensing everyone's eyes on her. Jebediah was staring with a puzzled expression, Gabe was grinning, Jobeth and Winnie had stopped what they were doing and turned to stare. Calico swallowed. "I need to feed the chickens before it gets too dark," she said stiffly, and glided from the room.

"And surely the mountain falling cometh to naught, and the rock is removed out of her place," Jobeth muttered beneath her breath as she watched Calico scoop up her jacket and slam out the door.

Winnie bristled. "Stick to quotin' Bible verses full of numbers, Jobeth, and leave off Job. Misquotin' him'll earn you passage right up to the devil's door." With that she turned her back and began to search over shelves for food to lay out a supper.

Sighing ostentatiously, Jobeth called to her son, "Let's be going, Gabe, your brothers'll all be hollering for their supper by now."

3

ONCE OUTSIDE, Calico snuggled deep into her thick jacket, giving no thought to her chickens. An excuse was all that comment had been, to get out from under the stilted glares and snide remarks she knew were being spoken even before she closed the door behind her. There was no moon that evening, nor were there any stars, only a gray blanket becoming rapidly darker as she followed the familiar path to the copse of dogwood on the scree.

The shroud of night brought with it the silky sounds of unseen creatures scurrying about the wood. Some, like her chickens fluttering to roost on the topmost limbs of trees surrounding the cabin, to nest. Others, like the opossum, skunk and raccoon, would be preening on the threshold of their burrows waiting for full darkness before venturing forth. As she approached the edge of the scree she looked back over her shoulder down into the dim hollow where the lonely cabin stood, seeing Jobeth and Gabe climbing into their old truck. Leaving. All the old hurt, the old pain, rose up within Calico, her knees went weak and she sat down upon the stump of an old log near her mother's grave.

She liked coming here. It was a healing sort of place. In her mind she often carried on dialogues with the two women buried beneath her feet—her mother and grandmother. Two women she'd neither seen, nor touched, nor hugged. They knew her painful secret and never revealed it, and they knew her shame and never chastised her. Often she asked them why it had to have happened to her. There was never an answer from those silent graves, but she imagined them listening and that counted for something.

It had not been easy for her as a child being raised by a man already bitter, already set in his ways. She had never been called cute or whimsical or sweet, had never had the softening touch of a woman's hand to guide her in dress or manner—or in the ways of men. Her heart rose in silent defence of her behavior centered about the strange man lying before the fire in the cabin, and she longed desperately for that guidance.

She sat on the stump until the wind began to whistle around her, tugging tendrils from her braid, making her fingers and nose numb from cold. Then an implacable force took hold and she knew she had to go back.

She strolled through the rear door and stood there a moment while the delicious aroma of Winnie's cookery wafted to her from stove and table. The old woman did not glance up as Calico removed her coat and hung it on a peg by the entrance, but Doc Willis gave her a swift penetrating look as he and Jebediah emerged from her room.

"We put him in your bed. Hope that's all right. If you don't think you can care for him, I'll come back and get him after I've got Christian down to the hospital in Gainsville."

"I can look after him," Calico said with utter calm, while every vital part of her beneath her skin burned with joy.

"You ought not to," Jebediah cautioned, looking over at her with a baleful expression as they sat down to table and the food Winnie had prepared. "You don't know what kind of a man he is... might be violent, escaped from prison... you don't know what all." The glare Calico cast over to him made his statement seem doubtful. Jebediah shrugged his once powerful shoulders. "Well...you hauled him from the river, reckon you know best."

Worry and doubt did not gnaw at Calico again until after dinner, when she stood by Doc Willis's van. Christian was lying inside on an improvised stretcher. "I ought to be going down to the hospital with him," she said.

"Be a waste of your time," the doctor said adamantly. "All he's going to do tonight is sleep—and maybe sober up some, too," he growled as an afterthought. "I'll operate tomorrow, get some skin over those exposed bones, and keep him plied with antibiotics. If there's any danger, any problems, I'll call Jeb, and let him know. You check with him, and I promise, if anything untoward happens, I'll send word or come myself."

"If you say so," she answered, still not entirely convinced, but relieved too, that she wouldn't suffer guilt for not following her grandfather down the mountain. Her heart, her mind, her soul were inside her own bedroom, lurking about the stranger where she felt her destiny lay.

Abraham Willis's old bones seemed to unhinge and snap back together as he climbed into his van and started the motor. "Oh, when your houseguest is ambulatory, send him on down to my office and I'll take out those stitches. And keep an eye on his stomach. If the skin begins to pucker up and look like grains of rice, get him to me at once, you hear?"

"What will it mean, his skin puckering?"

"Punctured lung. But it won't happen unless his rib shifts, which isn't likely—just precaution."

"What about that cut on his head?" Calico asked aloud, but the questioning in her silvery eyes took on an ominous glimmer in the lamplight filtering into the yard.

Doc Willis understood her inquiry. "If he wakes up with no sense it's 'cause he didn't have any afore he got banged on the head. You just keep infection from setting in on that leg. That splinter penetrated muscle. It's going to be mighty sore."

Winnie touched Calico's arm to get her attention. "I gave that pup a bowl of sausage stew. And don't worry about your grampa, me and Jeb'll see him to the hospital." She bent her lips close to Calico's ear, whispering, "You took to that man in there, ain't you?"

"Get into the truck, Winnie," Jebediah ordered, holding open the door, his interruption saving Calico from having to answer. He saw his wife settled, then turned back to Calico.

"You got a dangerous streak in you, Calico, just like your grampa. Don't go doing anything foolish. Christian did once and it cost him twenty years—twenty of the best years of his life."

Calico laughed, a feminine version of her grandfather's. "Jeb, I'm going to be helping a man back to health, not taking it away from him."

After everyone had gone the sudden stillness engulfed her. She felt so spent. Never did she want to live through another day like today. While she was standing in the yard, in the darkness, there came the tentative chirping of insects—too tentative, she decided. It meant more rain. Inertia held her immobile for another few minutes. She lifted her face to the wind, waiting to see if she sensed a presence, trusting her intuition to tell her if someone prowled the mountain. But there was no alarm, no skin prickling at the nape of her neck, no feelings beyond the oneness she felt with her ancestors up on the scree, so she turned to the cabin with the firm purposeful step of the indomitable.

4

IN HER ROOM Calico surveyed the man thoughtfully, speculatively, the fact of their aloneness dawning in her eyes. From the corner she pulled up a cane-back chair next to the feather bed, sitting in it with the lamp turned low, but not so low that it didn't cast a dim light over his face. She watched his every move, an eyelid twitching, his fingers curling around the quilt, his tongue flicking out to parched lips, which she then moistened with cool water.

Along about midnight he began to run a fever and in his delirium he chatted away. Some words were clear, others garbled, but she caught phrases and snippets... of his sister, Antonio, whom it sounded as though he didn't like, and there was Rose and Belle... she didn't like them, but she supposed a man such as he would have had women, lots of women.

Once when she was sitting on the side of the bed, trying to spoon water into his mouth he suddenly sat straight up, and grabbing her throat in his hands nearly throttled her to death, screaming all the while about a man named Gerald Vincent. And then as clear as day, he pronounced Vincent not worth it and released her neck, lying back down as calm as anything while she leaped up gasping for air, knowing there would be bruises on her face and neck come morning.

From then on she kept to the cane-back chair. At dawn the rain stopped and she woke with a start as a shaft of sunlight beamed through a crack in the curtains and slanted across her eyelids. She bathed his

face, then his wounds with cloths dipped in warm epsom salts.

Afterward she left his side to freshen herself so that
when he woke she would look presentable. She
brushed her hair, arranging it into a bun at the nape
of her neck, found it too severe, and began again. This
time she swept it atop her head, but didn't like that
either, and finally settled for her usual braid with vagrant wisps curling enchantingly about her ears. She
made coffee, fried sausages, eggs and biscuits. But the
stupid man refused to wake. She began to worry that
he might starve to death.

With a sigh she sat at his bedside once again and
began to hum; tunes she knew from church and
childhood, and still he didn't stir. She remembered
that when people were unconscious it was said you
should talk to them as if they understood you. So she
talked.

She told him all she knew about gold, the master
lure, the divine substance regarded by the ancients as
coming from the sun. She told him how to find it, to
chip it out of rock and how to slither along your belly
in an old mine and find a likely spot.

She explained how to crush rock and amalgamate
the gold with mercury, then the technique of burning
off the silvery metal leaving the gold wet, and how to
set it in the sun to dry. While she put fresh warm
cloths on his leg she told him the legend of the phi-
losophers' stone and how it was supposed to have the
power of changing common metals into precious gold
and silver, and about the Augustine monk, Wenzel
Seiler, and Emperor Leopold I who were said to have
changed a silver medal into gold in 1677. And when
the man responded to none of this, she bent close to
his ear and told him that if he didn't believe her, he
could go to Vienna to see the medal for himself. She
mentioned the 472-pound Holtermann nugget found

in Australia and how she wished she'd found it herself. Through all this storytelling he slept, and finally
she leaned back into her chair with resignation and
amused herself watching his beard stubble grow
darker on his lean strong jaw.

Then she renewed her efforts, keeping on doggedly,
telling him sacred myths of Talking Rock Mountain,
the foolery about the Spanish Treasure and how
Georgia had been the site of the first gold rush in the
United States in 1820, more than 160 years ago. She
told him that when gold was discovered in California
in 1849 all the miners left Georgia, which suited her
just fine, because now she was finding all the gold
they hadn't. She was hoarse by the time the sun was
at high noon, and disgusted, too. People loved to hear
her tell gold stories and she had told him every one
she could remember, but he hadn't shown the least bit
of interest. If anything, he was sleeping more soundly
than ever. Half-seriously, she began to wonder if she
was boring him and he was too well mannered to
wake up and tell her so.

Perhaps gossip would intrigue him. After moisten-
ing his lips, she took a sip of water and began telling
him of the people in her life and Lumpkin County.

There was her grampa who had killed a man and
spent twenty years in prison, and Winnie and Jebediah who had raised her daddy, McKenzie, while
grampa was in jail, and she told him about Jobeth
who was determined to have seven children because
seven was God's number, and how she picked out
only the names of saints and angels and named her
boys after them, which was as close to God as they
were ever likely to get, because they were hellions...
that Jobeth had had this all figured out from the time
she had read that God had ordered Noah to put every
clean beast into the Ark by sevens. But talking of Jobeth brought her closer to Judalon, and with a slice of

her hand in front of the unconscious face she cut off talk about people.

"The least you could do," she finally told him, weary with exasperation, "is wake up and tell me your name."

His eyelids fluttered and she got a glimpse of green through slitted lashes, then his mouth began to work, shaping a word. She put her ear to his lips hearing him gasp out, "Irish McCaulley." A small shock went through her and she stood rooted to the floor, momentarily transfixed. Her legs went weak as her heart vaulted in a fit of anticipation while her lungs suddenly turned to stone so that she couldn't breathe, but by now she was past all politeness and sympathy for what he had put her through.

"You nearly choked me to death," she blurted, then sagged on the chair as she watched him slip off again. Oh, he was cold-blooded, galling, and to think she had lost a night's sleep and talked herself hoarse for his benefit. Yet, as she went into the kitchen to make another pot of coffee, she said his name over and over again so that it became familiar to her tongue and she wouldn't stumble over it.

Nature was no more resolute than Calico, no more variable. As she ministered to her charge once again, her mind was a fiendish frenzy of inconsequential thoughts, none of which made any sense, though she told herself that she was beginning to hate the man lying amid the coccoon of warm coverlets on her bed.

Irish woke to being prodded and poked in private places, painful places. His eyes fluttered once, twice, testing the light, careful to make sure that the throbbing behind them remained bearable. Through heavily lidded eyes he saw smooth tanned skin, copper-colored hair and magnificent gray eyes that he knew from somewhere but were now inspecting him with aloof hostile interest. The face in which the eyes were lodged was an angular puzzle; parts that shouldn't fit together did, so that he couldn't tear his gaze away to look beyond the slender neck or the soft flesh at her jaw that was taut with tension. On another level he noted that his chest was bound in some manner, that he was naked, that his throat was parched, that his head ached like the devil and his right leg throbbed. It was abject misery.

"Don't conk out on me again," Gray Eyes said. "How do you feel?" Her voice was throaty, soft and sweet, so controlled that at first he didn't sense the strength and passion hidden beneath the surface. He gave her a weak smile that didn't quite come off.

"I was just thinking about that," he managed hoarsely. "Battered, but alive. I could use something to drink."

Calico knew she was being scrutinized and kept still for his exploring gaze. She liked his voice. It was deep and sensual, at odds with his irregular hawk-like features. "You rode an uprooted tree down the sluice," she told him. "Doc Willis sewed up your head, took a splinter out of your leg and said you have a broken rib."

"I remember it all," he shuddered, raising his head. His skull pounded like a jackhammer. "Er...miss, could I have that water? I've got a terrible thirst."

She jerked upright. "Yes. Oh! And coffee, too. I've made fresh." She hurried from the room, flustered now, filing everything about him in separate little corners of her brain for review when she was alone. He has extraordinary green eyes, she thought, and she liked the way his lips moved and formed around words.

A kaleidoscope of facts tripped through Irish's brain as he very carefully pulled himself into a sitting position. He had an odd feeling of disassociation, but it disappeared if he held his head still. Of course he wasn't in any hospital. He was knocked about some, but still in one piece. His hostess was abrupt, but he'd always heard these mountain people were a wary lot. He wondered about Sam, and then mindful of his head, cautiously reconnoitered his surroundings.

He was in an alcove of sorts, the low ceiling above his head presumably serving as a floor to a loft or another sleeping area. Against one whitewashed wall was a mahogany-and-oak bureau with a sloping hinged lid that could have matched anything put up for auction at Sotheby's or Christie's. Above the bureau was an ornately framed mirror so badly in need of glazing that it was rendered useless. There was an odd assortment of chests and trunks of the sort that one might find in any attic, but these were obviously in use. And this bed he was in—damned comfortable, he thought, felt like a cloud. Everything was scrupulously clean.

Her room, he concluded, as the girl returned bearing a wooden tray, and he was surprised to feel his heart accelerate as she bent near, since no woman had ever ignited his emotions upon a first meeting. He put the flapping of his insides down to the terrifying ordeal he had survived. She adjusted the tray over his thighs, retrieving one of the cups of steaming coffee as she sat in the cane-back chair. The water was cool and sweet, putting to rest his thirst, the coffee rid him of cobwebs that lingered in his brain. The girl watching him so covertly was an enigma. "Good coffee," he said. "What's your name?"

"I told you already. Calico Jones."

His eyebrow shot up. "You told me already? When?"

"Why... why... yesterday, this morning again. I talked you conscious," she told him, anxious that he realize what fine care she'd given him. "What are you doing on Talking Rock Mountain?"

He smiled ruefully. "Talked into it by a man with quick wit and a tremendous gift for influencing people."

"You talk in riddles," Calico accused, her face impassive, wanting specifics, yearning to know his age, his likes, his dislikes, his everything, and reluctant to ask anything so personal.

"A friend loaned me his cabin, perhaps you know him. Phillip Braeswood."

"Yes. Grampa leased him two acres on the other side of the mountain. What's your business up here?"

His mouth drew into a bitter line. "I just came up here to sort myself out."

Her hand flew to her neck, where bruises were beginning to show. "Did you have a fight with a man named Gerald Vincent?"

"How the hell do you know about that?" he asked stiffly, the expression on his face going glacier cold.

"You talked about it in your sleep. Once you thought I was him."

He noticed her hand fluttering at her neck, reached for it and pulled it away from a bruise. Appalled, he asked, "Did I do that?"

"You didn't mean to."

"I'm sorry." He finished off his coffee, then drew a hand over his chin, feeling beard stubble. Two days' growth, he thought, surprised, feeling suddenly awkward and out of place. Misplaced. "My dog, Sam. He's around?" he asked, and when she nodded, he continued, "I've intruded on you long enough. If I could have my clothes, and the use of your bathroom...?"

"Oh. You can't leave yet. You're not well." She removed the tray from his lap, setting it aside on the floor. "I'll get you some hot water to shave, and I'll help you to the toilet. It's a ways off the porch down the path. But I've got to check your stomach before you get up."

"What! Whoa, lady!" His hand shot out, grasping her wrist as she began to turn down the quilt.

Calico burned at the touch. "I'm just doing what Doc Willis said. I'm supposed to check your stomach for rice puffs in case you have a punctured lung."

"I don't have a punctured lung," he growled ominously, pushing her hand back to her side with a snap. "Believe me, if I had a hole in my lung I'd be bent over double with the pain of air in my chest cavity."

Calico's eyes narrowed. "How do you know?"

"Because I've studied medicine. Taught it, too," he added, and wished he hadn't because it brought back all the reasons he'd let Phillip Braeswood talk him into making this pilgrimage to find himself. What he needed to be doing was to be out looking for a job, a good medical school that promised him all the time he wanted for research. What he didn't need was something like this chit of a country bumpkin to complicate his life. He'd sworn off permanent liaisons since Belle's departure.

As if to reinforce his thoughts, he inspected Calico more closely, embracing the whole of her now—the tanned slender neck disappearing into a fitted poplin shirt pulled taut over rounded breasts, the small waist, belted, that flared into curvaceous hips, long legs encased in khakis that were tucked into boots laced precisely to her knee. Masculine attire, yet on her blatantly feminine. He fed words to himself like stoic and stolid to describe her, rejecting them in favor of graceful, seductive and earthy and they weren't quite right either. Damn, but he was drawn to her. "You live here alone?"

Her color heightened. "No, with my grandfather. He—"

"Never mind," he said, waving away her answer, as he swung his legs over the bedside, dragging quilts and wincing with pain and nausea that shot through him.

"Let me help—"

"No. No!" He pushed her hands away. "I'll be all right. I've got to get back over to my cabin. No one knows where I am."

"Who would come looking?"

"Anybody," he snapped through clenched teeth, sighing heavily as he managed to sit upright with his bare feet firmly planted on the floor. "Thank your grandfather for hauling me out of the river, will you. And I'll cover the doctor's fees." Bending slowly to ease the pain in his chest, he ran his hand over his calf, feeling stiches, counting ten. "Damned leg hurts like hell."

"My grampa didn't pull you out of the river. I did," she told him loftily. "You can thank me." He couldn't leave just like this. She had to stop him. But no way came to mind. Her heart sagged, seeing the measuring, skeptical expression on his face.

"There's a whole lot more of me than there is of you, lady. You don't expect me to believe you pulled me from the river, all by your lonesome?" He laid on the sarcasm. She was taking him for a fool but that bump he'd taken on his head hadn't knocked out all the sense he owned.

The color drained from her cheeks. "You don't believe me."

"I'm not in a position to contradict you," he said smoothly. All he wanted now was to get back to civilization, to Atlanta, where rivers didn't sneak up on you and where he could tell by the gleam in her eye what any redhead he met had on her mind. God! But his head hurt.

"You think I'm lying! I can tell by the tone of your voice, the way you're looking at me." She felt despair. She'd never had to press for credibility. Just the opposite, playing down tales told on her, curbing exaggerations when she could. Irish McCaulley just didn't understand that the mountain had brought them together.

"I appreciate your taking care of me," he said, but she wasn't placated. Anger coursed through her. This man was no gift from the mountain. He was nothing more than a piece of refuse. And unappreciative, no matter how smooth talking. The river hadn't give him up, it had thrown him back!

"I thought you were set apart from other men," she said with utter honesty.

He gave her a sharp glance, one eyebrow raised inquiringly. "Set apart from other men? A strange thing to say. In what way?"

She could think only of escape. "None of your business! Your old dog is under the kitchen sink. He's been fed, and your clothes—what's left of them—are on the back porch." She scooped up the Jergen's jars in which she hid her gold cache, stalking from the room, her pride drooping somewhere down around her ankles.

She would go to town, do her laundry, stop by the hospital to see grampa, then pick up her mail from the post office. As for the stranger, he could find his own way off the mountain, and into the river again for all she cared. She stored her gold in the glove compartment of her truck, then staunchly retrieved her purse from her room, ignoring the stumbling man as if he no longer existed.

"What was your name again...Calico! That's it. Wait a minute." He was talking to air. He swore out loud as he heard the engine rev and roar as the truck sped down the mountain. Eyes closed, he clung to the bedpost cursing, inhaling deep breaths, finding no relief from his tightly bound chest.

There was a flannel robe hanging on a hook; he

shrugged into it. Too tight across his shoulders, he discovered, so he took it off and tied it instead around his hips to cover his nakedness and made his way to the back porch. Sam followed him out.

The air had a tang to it, an unmistakable bouquet of pine and mud and damp earth and chicken droppings. Ranged over a trestle secured to the wall he found a bar of Lava soap, towels, cloths, a chipped basin and a pitcher of icy water, toothbrushes and toothpaste. He squeezed out toothpaste onto his finger and cleaned his teeth, and using the icy water, went no further in his ablutions than was necessary.

He spotted a rumpled mass that he recognized as his clothes lying on the floor, and holding them up to the sunlight, let loose a string of expletives. They were cut to shreds, still filled with mud and sand and sopping wet. One of his favorite crew necks and a forty-dollar pair of slacks! His head throbbed unmercifully. With two fingers he explored tenderly the gash, tracing lightly and counting the stitches. Eleven! He'd have a bald spot and a scar for weeks to come.

Then, because he could put it off no longer, he limped barefoot down the path to the outhouse, steadfastly watching where he put his feet to avoid chicken droppings and becoming more and more appalled at the primitive environment in which he found himself. Only a thin wisp of smoke curling from a neighboring mountain betrayed another human presence.

When he returned to the cabin, Sam elected to remain out of doors. As Irish stood on the threshold of the vast main room, he felt a maddening loneliness descend upon him for no apparent reason. He shook his head to dispel the feeling and regretted it immediately. He would willingly trade a year of his life for two aspirins.

The house he now noticed was well furnished,

clean with a comfortable lived-in look. Easy to imagine it pictured in some magazine touting early Americana. Too early for his taste! He rummaged through the second bedroom and found clothes of sorts—pants, shirt, socks, old boots, none of which fit properly, but he tugged them on anyway. He would package them up and return them with a check when he got back to Atlanta.

He stepped onto the front porch and whistled for Sam. "Come on boy, let's head back to . . . ." The words died in his throat as he pivoted slowly. If he'd been a crying man, he would have hung his head and bawled. He hadn't the slightest idea where he was, or more precisely—where his cabin was located, or how far. Dejected, he sat down on the steps in the warm sun, and that's where Calico found him when she returned.

She whipped the truck around in the yard and backed up to the steps so that he had to jump out of the way of the tailgate. She set the brake, got out and came around to the rear of the truck and began unloading sacks of canned goods, and the baskets of tumbled dried and folded clothes.

"Good God! Didn't you see me sitting there? You almost ran me over. I could've been killed!" he ground out, cursing the luck that had driven him into the camp of this unwilling hostess.

Her face unreadable, Calico looked him up and down, once, twice as though this was the very first time she'd ever laid eyes on him. "I could've just left you in the river, too." She pushed past him into the house, arms filled with groceries.

"Ah, hell, lady. You take your vitamins, and have the strength of an amazon. I concede the fact that you, and none other, hauled me from a watery death. Good enough?" She flicked a look of contempt over her shoulder. "Not good enough, obviously," he mut-

tered, and when she reemerged onto the porch again
he said: "Gee, I just love Southern hospitality." Every
word dripped with his particular brand of sarcasm.
He was old-fashioned in his ideas of women, and it
showed. It was that instinctive male primeval curse—
or compensation?—deposited into the species from
the day God borrowed a rib from Adam. Calico honed
in on it, harassing him like a descendant of Scylla.
And she was just as skilled as he in polite sarcasm.

She smiled sweetly. "I didn't notice you traipsing in
here with a written invitation." Her unique features
were set in an unyielding wall, and Irish knew he was
going to have to swallow his pride and ask for help. It
galled him.

"If you could point in the direction of Phillip's
place, I'll be more than happy to be on my way," he
told her, his tone cold and positive.

She waved a hand airily toward the east. "Fifteen
minutes walk, you'll be there."

The forest she so casually indicated looked shadowy and menacing. He liked pavements, buildings,
streets and maps, so you knew where you were, knew
what was around the corner, knew what to expect.
"That close?" he said with deceptive indifference.
"Perhaps you'd like to stroll over with me? I could
change into my own clothes and return these—save
me from having to mail them back."

The quicksilver eyes turned on him and seemed to
ignite.

Irish trailed behind as Calico topped a slight rise
and looked down at Phillip Braeswood's cabin in the
tiny clearing bordering the river. A white sports car
was parked only yards from the door, which swung
back and forth in the wind. Sam raced ahead, yipping
and barking at unseen challenges as she waited pa-
tiently for Irish to limp to her side. "Did you leave the
door open when you left?" she asked.

"I know I closed it. I don't remember locking it. I wasn't exactly expecting to take a swim. I'd heard the river gurgling all night and just stepped out during a break in the storm to take a look." He pointed to a gully across the river. "I watched that tree lose its hold in the earth and come rushing down that cut. Next thing I knew it had plowed into the river and slammed into the bank on this side, knocking me into the water." Everything about the clearing looked serene now. "You think something's wrong?"

"I don't know. I don't like that door being ajar like that. You stay here until I check it out."

"The hell with that!" he exploded. "I'm not hiding behind a woman's skirt." He longed for the contentment of his laboratory, his work, then recalling how Gerald Vincent had backed him into a corner and fired him, he sighed. If he'd ever wondered, he was sure of it now. God didn't like him. Six years of his life wasted, working at Bateman with the promise of tenure less than a year away.

"I hardly ever wear a skirt," Calico said tersely, giving him a "suit yourself" look as she started down the rise with Irish on her heels. He winced as the muscle in his injured leg screeched with angry pain each time he put his foot down.

She was first through the door. The cabin was in total disarray. It had the look of a vandal at work and Calico knew just who that vandal would be.

Irish brushed past her, came to a dead halt and gaped, a look of outrage stretching across his craggy features. His nostrils flared with anger. He threw the wad of damp clothes he'd carried under his arm against the wall. "No wild animal did this!" he bellowed. His suitcase had been dumped and scattered, the two-foot-high stack of folders that listed grants available and teaching institutions to which he might apply were scattered like confetti about the polished floor. Calico watched him out of the corner of her eye as he began to roam the room, picking up his precious papers, moaning and groaning with the effort as he bent over.

"All my food's gone!" He was mad, boiling.... "I'm going to file a report with the police. A—"

"No!" she protested with feeling.

He spun around and glared at her. "The hell you say no! I'm filing a report. I don't like people stealing from me."

"This is my mountain. I said no." Her jaw thrust out stubbornly, her eyes glittering with what he couldn't tell, but clarity dawned on him.

"You know who did this! You know and you're protecting someone!" He shot across the room, grabbing her shoulders, his fingers biting into soft flesh. "Listen here, little lady, you can just make a trip into town with me and tell the sheriff what you know. I'll be damned if I'll let somebody get away with this."

She held her tongue until he turned her loose and stomped painfully over to where his wet clothes had fallen in a heap at the base of the wall. Picking them up, he began digging into the pockets. The thick wad in the back pocket he'd assumed was his wallet was mud. In rapid succession he turned out the rest of the pockets, scattering sand and gravel as he did. "Where the hell is my wallet? My car keys?" He looked to her with the question.

She gave an elegant shrug of her shoulders. "If they were in your pocket when you went in the river, then they're in the river now—doubtful you'll ever find them."

He let loose a string of vituperation and expletives. Calico stood like stone with her heart thudding. He couldn't leave! It was too wondrous to contemplate. "You might spot them when the river goes clear again," she said doubtfully. "If they ended up in shallow water, that is. On the other hand, the river winds around the mountain for about four miles before it feeds into the Chestatee. . . ." Her voice trailed off, but she had injected just the right amount of sympathy.

"That's not practical and you know it. Think I'm stupid?"

"Never once thought that," she replied blandly. "Don't you have a second set?"

"Sure I do. Hanging next to a pot holder in my kitchen in Atlanta. Fat lot of good they'll do me there."

"It's not the end of the world. I'll help you straighten up things here, and I can drive you to Atlanta when my grandfather gets out of the hospital. I can't leave until I know for certain he's okay. What do you want to take with you?"

"Take with me where?" he asked in confusion, dazed in the manner in which only the most precise, the most orderly of people can be.

"Back to my place, of course. You can't stay here. There's no food."

"Will you drive me into town to the police?"

"No."

He hesitated before replying, drawing his hand over his face in a weary gesture of acquiescence, and slowly turning about the room. "I'm between a rock and a hard place," he sighed finally. "Okay, let's go."

Calico hated Judalon Tarrant, and this vandalism had his stamp all over it, but for one reluctant moment she was willing to offer him a sideways thank-you.

5

THEY WERE ALMOST BACK to her cabin, Calico carrying his vintage suitcase while Irish limped along, struggling with a cardboard box. The box was filled to its brim with the papers and folders they'd gathered from the floor. Each time he'd picked one up Irish had muttered, "This might be my future, or this...or this one," until he sounded like a broken record. He had not come out of his foul mood. Country life wasn't for him. Falling into a damned river was not his idea of a quiet interlude in which to think and plan his career, or having to be under the thumb of a redheaded viper, regardless of how attractive. As they walked single file across the scree, Irish noticed the crosses. It was just like these people to hold onto their dead, he thought, burying them practically on their doorstep. "Quaint little graveyard you have there," he said.

It was the way he said it, the condescending tone in his voice that made the remark flippant. He had moved across her special boundary. Calico whirled, gray eyes smoldering, blocking his path.

"Quaint! *Quaint*? Those graves aren't quaint, they're sacred!" she flung at him. "My mother's and my grandmother's...I'm fed up with you—you interloper, you arrogant goat, you skinny cavalier! What gives you the right to go around being so patronizing and calling people names?" She gesticulated wildly with her free hand, emphasizing her words.

They glared at one another, toe to toe, each an implacable warrior until Calico suddenly grabbed his

jacket sleeve, yanking him down the scree in a fast
trot so that Irish was hard put to balance and hang
onto his precious papers and favor his injured leg all
the same time. His chest was heaving against its bind-
ing, his leg jerking with painful spasms when she finally turned him loose at the river's edge. "You have
no pity... no pity," he gasped, sucking in air.

"Pity! I'll tell you pity." She slammed his suitcase
into the mud. "Right here...! This is where that tree
was, you were caught up in it—your dog brought you
to my attention. And I came down here and pulled
you out. Right there." She pointed to the exact spot,
daring him to dispute her. "Later I dragged you up
that hill to my house and laid you out in front of the
fire. I cut off your clothes... and let me tell you something. I haven't seen many men, but I don't think
you're anything special—" She had never before seen
a naked man, if you didn't count Jobeth's boys when
they were babies, but that didn't matter now. Irish
was blushing for perhaps the second time in his life.

"Then I cleaned your wounds and sent a friend for
Doc Willis. I wasn't in no mood to keep messing with
you either, because I'd just spent the second worst
hour of my life trying to keep my grampa from bleed-
ing to death." By now her fury was so great she was
choking on the words. "You're a stranger and you're
in a pickle—none of which is my fault, but I'm offering you mountain hospitality. If you don't want it—
why, there's the road'll take you down to the highway where you can hitch a ride to wherever it is you
want to be. And you've never even said thank-you,
not sincerely, you haven't."

He was knocked off center, staring at Calico for a
stunned few seconds, every part of him rigid with
control. No woman had ever taken this tone with
him. Angry, the girl before him had a wild erotic look,
she was biting on her lower lip as if to hold back

another tirade. She struck a deep well that he'd thought had gone dry long ago, and he became aware that he'd been without a woman for a very, very long time. He inhaled the delicate scent of lilies that projected in his mind's eye the nymph that moved about his unconscious. "Er, look, la—" he began, stopping when she thrust her face nearer his.

"My name is Calico Jones—you got that? I'm not *lady*. It sounds like something you'd call a dog."

There was a spark of warmth in his green eyes, a mere trace of a smile on his lips. "I believe I've got that," he said softly. "I accept your hospitality."

Feet spread apart on the spongy earth, hands on her hips, she eyed him with skepticism, certain that he was concealing something behind soft words. "You're sure about that?" She hadn't meant to sound so caustic, now that things were going her way.

He gave her a curt nod of apology, which was painful enough—both for his throbbing head and for his pride. "Calico Jones," said Irish, deliberately, savoring the feel of the name on his tongue, finding that he liked it. "I'm Nathan McCaulley."

"You told me your name was Irish."

His lips twisted slightly. "Irish is my nickname, on account of my temper tantrums."

He's mocking me just as sure I'm standing here with the river ebbing at my feet and the wind cutting me clear through, she reflected. Grabbing up his suitcase, she strode determinedly up the hill, tossing back over her shoulder, "Just you be sure to ask my permission before you go throwing any fits on my mountain."

He lingered behind, watching the way her lithe body rippled beneath her khakis, becoming aware of a sensation in his loins and that his arms were growing weary from the weight of the box. He hobbled like a one-legged spear thrower to catch up to her. "A bit on the arrogant side yourself, aren't you, Miss Jones?"

"I'm home, you're not," said Calico, the barb a rapier unsheathed.

He dropped back. It was a comment that hit hard. He had lived in many places, travelling over the globe, but had never been home in the exacting sense of that word. He had no roots, desiring them above most things. He knew of his mother, Rose McCaulley, carrying her name, but nothing of the man who had fathered him, and it ate at his pride like a growing cancer. Unadoptable and unwanted, that was him. He watched Calico disappear into the cabin, wondering why, in spite of all she'd done and said, he still felt so drawn to her. She belonged to this mountain, to those ancestors of hers up there on the scree, to the grandfather she'd mentioned. That was it. She belonged. He had never belonged anywhere. It was as though he was forever standing outside looking in—and he wanted desperately to be inside. He felt the warm stirring in his loins once again. With a start he realized he wanted to be inside *her* house, *her* life, *her* body. And then told himself he was a fool even to think it.

His gaze swept over the wild mountain, the trees she had identified for him—pine, poplar, sweet gum and white oak—swaying in the sun-gentled breeze, seeming to beckon him. The landscape didn't appear so forbidding after all.

"THERE ARE BETTER PLACES to live than Atlanta, believe me," said Irish as he spread the contents from the cardboard box on the table.

"But I like Atlanta," objected Calico. "Our favorite place used to be the Biltmore Hotel at 817 West Peachtree. Do you know it? After we had checked in, grampa would take me across the street to Fan and Bill's for lobster newburg, and there was ice...ice everywhere—in tea, soft drinks, buckets in our room."

"Fan and Bill's is gone and the Biltmore is being turned into a condominium."

"I know," she said, sounding wistful. "That's why we don't go to town anymore." She was cooking supper, stealing looks at Irish every chance she got and thinking that it was a good thing the thoughts she was having weren't visible. Though she disliked admitting it, she was a novice at love affairs. She told herself it didn't matter because she knew what she wanted and she knew who. He was sitting at one end of the dining table engrossed in sorting his papers and making lists. Every now and then he ran his hand through his thick curly black hair or touched his fingers to his temple. He had shaved, changing into his own clothes—gray slacks, a black turtleneck sweater—and she was wondering how old he was.

She was also pondering their first kiss, anticipating it, a special kiss—the kind that makes cymbals crash, bugles trumpet and butterflies march. She was working fifteen feet away from him at the cookstove, but it might as well have been two inches, for she was aware each time his eyes bore into her back. It was like an electric probe, generating an undercurrent of excitement that was tangible in the air.

Every time she turned her back, Irish stared at her in wonder, uncontrollably stirred by a sensual promise he couldn't ignore. A lamp hanging on a chain from a ceiling beam cast a bewitching glow over her, highlighting the copper in her auburn hair that lay in a thick braid along her spine. The pungent odor of the kerosene lamp, the sharper smell of pine resin as it caught fire and shot up the chimney, the delicious aromas emanating from the stove and the scent of lilies when Calico brushed past him setting the table, all combined to evoke images of sensual pleasure. His concentration was shot to hell. If he didn't get off this mountain, he'd never find work.

An uneasy silence lay between them by the time Calico was dishing up venison sausage, boiled new potatoes, biscuits and freshly baked cake. She couldn't stand it. "I didn't really mean what I said about you," she said as she passed him butter and a jar of honey.

"Oh, which particular thing was that? You've said a number of them," he pointed out with feeling.

"About when I cut your clothes off...." His eyebrow shot up, her heart sank. She was going about this all wrong. "What I mean is, I don't really think you're ugly. I mean...."

"No harm done," he said.

"Well, I didn't expect that I'd done any harm," she sniffed. They were nearly finished with supper before she had the courage to speak again. "You're from up north, aren't you? You don't sound Southern."

"Boston. I was raised in an orphanage." He surprised himself mentioning something that he usually held secret. Belle had thrown it in his face all during their marriage, saying she'd only married him because it was her year to give to charity. The fury he had felt then was coming on him, wire taut. He attempted to deflect it, changing the subject. "You're a good cook, Calico. That was the best meal I've eaten in months."

She flushed with pleasure. "Did it hurt your feelings, being put in an orphanage?"

"That's none of your business." His squarely built pride, a guardhouse for his emotions, would never allow him to admit such a weakness.

Calico recognized a stubborn man when she saw him. But whether she liked it or not, and sometimes she didn't, she was of these mountains with all their old-fashioned customs and rituals, and she couldn't go about kissing a man who tried to remain a mystery. "You talked about Rose and Belle in your sleep," she persisted, changing the subject in the hope of drawing him out. "Who are they?"

His eyes flashed something akin to anger as though she had penetrated some hidden well, something secluded, never to be dredged up for the perusal of others. "Do you have any aspirin? My head's beginning to throb." He pushed his plate away. "I'd like to turn in. Where am I bunking down?"

Calico sighed inwardly. She could be just as stubborn as he. She'd drag the answers out of him eventually. She had to, but perhaps now wasn't the time. She got him the aspirins, poured him fresh coffee and directed him to her grandfather's room, watching him as he limped forward and closed the door firmly behind himself.

The food in her stomach settled like lead. So Irish McCaulley had boundaries, too. She gave up all thoughts of kissing. Tomorrow was a new day, and as she lay in her bed that night, Calico plotted it like a general on the verge of battle.

The following morning Irish hurt all over and he couldn't walk, not without her help. Calico was thrilled. "I'll serve you breakfast in bed," she declared, delighted with this opportunity to wait on him once more. All her life she had been only as domestic as necessary, cooking because she had to eat, washing clothes and dishes to render them useful once again, but this was different, and now she gloried in being domesticated.

But Irish would have no part of it. "The hell with that. Hand me my robe."

"You ought to let me bathe your leg in epsom salts first, then you'd enjoy your breakfast more."

"What are you smiling at?" he shot at her, his expression glum.

"I'm not smiling. It's a nice day out, not too cold,

maybe an Indian summer after this cold snap. Let me help you with your robe.''

He declined, biting his lip to hold back a groan. His ribs were aching too. He had no choice but to accept her help to the outhouse, muttering about primitives, suffering mortification, while Sam trotted back and forth, scattering chickens in his path.

As the day progressed Calico was conscious of a wild exhilaration. It was impossible for two people thinking the way they were to spend time together cooped up in the comfortable cabin without having certain ideas. Each caught the other staring, and then glanced quickly away. Calico thought it was wonderful and began planning her kiss again.

After several warm Epsom-salts baths the swelling in his leg went down and Irish thought he might be able to walk again, but this remained only a thought. He had never allowed anyone to wait on him before, but Calico insisted and he again accepted her help to move to the sofa where he propped up his leg on a foot-stool. She brought him stack after stack of his sorted papers, and every now and then he would call out asking what she thought of this grant or that teaching institution. Calico knew little, but she learned to nod as if giving it thought and then ask; ''What do you think?'' while carefully listening for a negative sound in his voice. Then she'd say, ''It doesn't sound up to your standards, does it?''

Anything that would take him away from Talking Rock wasn't up to hers and she delighted each time he answered, ''No, I don't think it is,'' and scratched that one from his list.

He had a dark shadow on his jaw by dinner and insisted on shaving even if he couldn't dress. Calico held her small round makeup mirror for him and once when he touched her fingers to adjust it, she nearly jerked her hand away. His touch was electric.

They ate on a small table she set up before the fire.

"Would to God I knew who took all my stuff," Irish said, suddenly wrathful. "I need a drink and the thief got two bottles of my best bourbon."

"You a drinker?" she asked, alarmed. She tolerated her grampa's penchant for spirits, even took a sip herself now and then, but a drinking man...that was a flaw she didn't want in her man.

"Moderate," he answered, looking at her quizzically.

Calico sighed. "My grampa keeps peach brandy, will that do?"

"Sounds good," he replied. She poured him a generous glass.

Irish took a swallow and felt the whiskey burn like smoking grit down to his belly. He choked and coughed, his eyes watered and he looked at Calico as if she'd given him poison.

"It—it never affects grampa like that," she stuttered. "My cousin Jeb makes it, he cooks it down in a copper pot. Grows his own peaches, too."

"Your grampa must have a lead-lined stomach," he gasped, wiping his eyes.

"There's blackberry wine if—"

"This will do. It just took me by surprise. Must be over a hundred proof." Calico was staring at him and this time when their eyes met, she didn't look away. "Why are you looking at me like that?" he asked.

"I've never met anyone without folks before— ever. Family, no matter how remotely connected in these foothills, always step in whenever there's a tragedy so children have a home."

The brandy had mellowed him, and the day just past had been pleasant. He felt nudged to give her some answer. "I know of my mother, her name was Rose. She died a few weeks after I was born."

Rose, Calico thought, that would be the Rose he'd

mentioned in his sleep. She wanted to press him about Belle, but didn't dare, hoping he would tell her on his own. "What about your daddy?"

"I don't know the first thing about him."

"Not even his name? Haven't you ever looked for him?"

Irish took a good swig of brandy before answering. "No, why should I?" He stared trancelike into the flickering fire, seeming detached from his surroundings. Visiting his past, thought Calico, leaning forward to catch his next softly murmured words, "When I was a child I always thought he'd show up. Then I'd worry that he'd come looking for me and I wouldn't be there... just kid stuff, like every other orphan wonders about his past and his parents."

"But, that's it!" she exclaimed suddenly. "That explains it. You're still wondering." She felt as if she'd solved a puzzle.

He darted a glance at her. "What makes you say that?"

"You leave signs. You insisted on leaving a note thumbtacked to the door of your cabin saying where you'd be. We're the only two people on the mountain. I thought that strange behavior. I put it down to the bump on your head. I understand now. You think your daddy might still come looking."

"You like to pry, don't you?" he said, his green eyes filling with scorn.

Her mouth went dry. She had somehow crept up to that boundary, that line he seemed to let no one cross. "You want more brandy? Or some coffee and a slice of cake?" she asked quickly, trying to keep her tone light.

"All I want is to get back to civilization," he snapped at her, his voice harsh.

Calico obeyed her first impulse. She jumped to her feet, placing her clenched fists on her hips, her anger rising like a living thing. "I wish you would go back to civilization! You can't go twenty minutes without barking or complaining about something. You're mean and nasty mannered. Not once have you said thank-you or please. I should've left you to ride that tree all the way down to the Chestatee River and let some other fool have the dubious honor of hauling you back from the edge of hell." She pivoted on her heel, propelled by anger to the front door, where she grabbed a jacket off a peg and slammed out.

Up on the scree she sat on the stump, dropped her chin into her hands and stared at the ground beneath her feet. *Oh, momma, if only you had lived! If only there was some way you could tell me what I'm doing wrong... tell me how to coax this stubborn man off his pride.* Calico was feeling wretched enough to cry.

"Ah! Here you are. I wondered where you'd wandered. I should've guessed after the reaming out you gave me. Your sacred place." Calico converted her slight start at Irish's appearance into an icily impersonal stare. Not toward him, but toward the crest of Springer Mountain lying in the darkening shadows far to the east.

"You're right, you know," he continued, his tone somehow a little softer. "I have been behaving like an ass. I'm sorry." Out of the corner of her eye she contemplated him, betraying no emotion, yet feeling the formless wanting that plagued her take shape, gaining substance with his nearness, so that it was becoming a tangible quality that she could almost reach out and touch.

"Did you want something?" she said finally.

He gave a small laugh and sat down on the stump next to her. It wasn't a very big stump, and they were shoulder to shoulder, thigh to thigh. Calico didn't dare move. She was remembering the feel of her naked breasts on his bare chest that first night.

"I'm longing for a shower or a bath. How do I go about it?" *What I really want is you,* he thought, feeling a visceral need for her that was so far beyond any sexual drive he'd ever experienced that he was trembling.

Calico felt him shivering. She herself was now hardly conscious of the evening coolness, although gooseflesh was erupting on her arms and legs. It was rather like the feeling she got when she was sitting in church and the soloist hit the high notes of "Amazing Grace". The sensation seemed to lock a warmth in her loins, and the spicy smell of his after-shave was intoxicating. "We have a hip tub behind the stove," she replied. "I'll roll it out and fill it for you, but what about your bandages?"

"They'll get wet." He was leaning closer, his arm slipping around her shoulder, then he was pulling her into him, his lips brushing the high curve of her cheekbone. He exerted a guiding pressure on her shoulder and they rose in unison to their feet.

His lips were everywhere. Calico closd her eyes, savoring every tiny tentative touch of his mouth until it closed over hers. He tasted of coffee and brandy and chocolate cake and smelled of Old Spice that was somehow just him, and she had time to inhale a bare gasp of air as his tongue thrust and sought hers, then she was meeting him, opening to him, enchanted, moving across clouds and Jobeth's prophecy was coming true with everything exploding up inside her; a white-hot fire streaking down her nerves, enveloping her entire body, so that she couldn't talk and her breath seemed to be pulsating in her throat. Irish pushed her away from him just to look at her in the moonlight, making sure she was no apparition and she whispered shamelessly, "Please, don't stop."

Her soft words and warm fragrant breath excited him more as the tip of her tongue found its way to the thick cord stretched taut in his neck, and he pulled her tighter into his arms against his lean solid body, hard and uncompromising, straining with utter want, longing coursing through him like some dormant disease frantic to surface.

"I hear them...I hear them..." she whispered against his lips.

"What?" he murmured hoarsely, unwilling to give up this sweetness to words when so much else was happening.

"The cymbals, the bugles and the butterflies marching," she said breathlessly.

His hands roamed beneath her jacket, cupping soft breasts quivering with desire, and as he nibbled on her lips he told her he saw lights, exploding lights swinging back and forth and that was when Calico heard the truck.

"Someone's here," she said, too entranced to speak above a whisper, aching to remain in his arms, but pushing him gently away. She tilted her head, listening and recognized the sound of the flapping tailgate. "It's Jobeth," she told Irish, her voice rising in surprise.

"Who? Send her on her way," he suggested throatily, dropping his arms reluctantly so that she stood free.

"Jobeth. My friend, the one who believes seven is God's number. I told you about her."

"No, I don't recall." The moon made a path across Calico's face, and Irish gave her a rare smile with nothing held back. "I suppose you told me when I was unconscious. The only thing I remember is you, as a naked mountain nymph."

The tiniest crib of laughter bubbled up in Calico's throat. "The only naked mountain nymph around here is Echo, and she pined away until only her voice remained." The twin beams of the truck were fully upon them. Feeling bold, she said teasingly, "I remember you naked, too."

"Is that a fact? And I remind you of—"

She turned away, smiling, slowing her pace down the scree so that he could keep up. "Chaos," she said and ran ahead, leaving him to limp behind, as she saw Jobeth step from the truck. Perhaps there was a message from Doc Willis about her grampa.

Watching her race forward to greet her friend, Irish's mind raced with the speed of light hunting for the definition of Chaos, and when he found it, shook his head. Chaos was the vast deep and confusion out of which came the earth and the gods and all other things. He knew he could never be that to anyone because the inside of him was a void surrounded by a great wall of pride and if he lost that....

6

"I DON'T KNOW who else I can ask," Jobeth said plaintively. She was agitated, her brassy red hair frizzed around her head like an out-of-control halo. Her wide freckled face was splotchy and her eyes red and swollen from crying. "Gabe and Frank, they can take care of themselves. Winnie's got the two middle boys, but I—can't you take Rafe and Mikie? Just bathe 'em and bed 'em down? I'll pick them up in the morning before school."

"What about your mother?" Calico asked, every fiber of her body protesting the invasion of her privacy, protesting against baby-sitting when there was this new, exciting relationship with Irish McCaulley to be explored and continued. She flicked her tongue out. The taste of him lingered on her lips. Out of the corner of her eye she saw Irish limp down the scree and skirt the cabin to the backyard. He acted funny every time he had to use the outhouse, as if it was an uncivilized sin.

"Pa sold twenty-five head of hogs and took ma to Las Vegas for their forty-seventh anniversary. They only decided to go for sure this morning after she got reservations in one of those fancy hotels—room 777."

Calico pressed her fingertips to her temples. "Numbers! Everything is numbers to you, Jobeth. The Bible is numbers, gambling is numbers, bingo is numbers. You can't live your whole life according to some number in—oh foot! Why? Just tell me why you need anyone to watch the boys on a school night—all night?"

Jobeth glanced once at her sons huddled against the seat and, tugging at Calico's coat sleeve, pulled her out of earshot. "It's Judalon. He's in jail over in Gainsville. He got a hold of liquor somewhere and he got into a fight. I've got to go bond him out." Calico's stomach gave a slight jolt. Jail. Where Judalon belonged. "One night in jail won't kill him. Why can't you wait until morning?"

"You don't understand. Judalon can't stand being cooped up. You know how big he is, hemmed in like that he's like a wild man. If I don't get him out tonight he'll...it'll be hard—" She turned her eyes away from Calico. Her hands caressed her stomach protectively. "It ain't been easy living with him all these years. And...and...I need to borrow $112." Jobeth's voice dropped to an anguished whisper.

Loathing shivered through Calico with a coldness that was depressing. She rubbed her hands along her arms to ward off the chill and lifted her silvery gray eyes to the mountain. The cool wind blowing across the river formed mists that swirled and rose among promontories that jutted out from the face of the mountain like lonely stone gods. Money? For Judalon? She couldn't. No! It went against everything she knew to help a man who was a thief and worse. Jobeth was talking, drawing her out of her momentary reverie.

"I ain't never asked you for anything, not in all these years, have I?" the woman almost whined. "It goes against my pride to have to ask, it's like...like begging."

"Jobeth, if you needed money for food, for yourself, for the children, I'd let you have it in a minute, but—"

Jobeth's head angled up, studying Calico's face in the lantern light ebbing from the cabin. There was stubbornness etched into that particular cachet to her features. "You want Judalon in jail, don't you?" she said with dawning clarity. "You're punishing him 'cause he married me instead of you! Oh, I knowed it. I knowed it all along." She put her work-worn hands to her face in abject misery.

"My God!" exclaimed Calico in horror. "Jobeth. No. I'll give you the money. Just don't think that. Don't ever say that." She left Jobeth standing in the yard while she went to count out the money, needing the moment alone in the cabin to compose herself. Mikie and Rafe were standing beside their mother when she returned.

"Here's the boys' pajamas and school clothes," said Jobeth, thrusting a paper sack at Calico. "You boys be good, you hear?"

"We will, ma," they chorused.

Rafe was a solemn seven-year-old with curly blond hair, deep brown eyes and having a quiet authority beyond his years. It was impossible to tell what he was thinking. If he told you, you knew; if he didn't, there was no guessing. Mikie, too, was blond, his eyes a deeper hue than Rafe's. The baby of his family, he had the sense to know the days remaining to him in this choice position were numbered. From his five older brothers he had learned how to be mean, coy, spiteful, stubborn, hateful and adorable, and he had an incredible affinity for knowing when to be what. He could read and cipher better than his pa, and made sure everyone knew it, which did not endear him to Judalon. He repeated everything he heard a grown-up say, so that no remark was safe or secret. As soon as he emerged into the cabin behind Calico and Rafe, he spied Irish warming his backside in front of the fire and surged forward to attack. "Are you the man the mountain belched up for Calico?"

"I beg your pardon?" said Irish, startled, looking down at the thigh-high towhead, then to the other side of the room where Calico had begun to trim the wick on a lamp. She put a match to it and the glow dispelled shadows at the rear of the cabin. Their eyes met, messages were exchanged and Irish muttered forlornly, "Ah, damn."

"Are you the man the mountain belched up for Calico?" Mikie repeated, slightly exasperated, and pointing to Calico. "Her."

"Er . . . I fell in the river, Calico pulled me out. . . ."

Mikie shook his head in disbelief. "How can a man fall into an itty bitty river? Indian ghosts pushed you?"

Irish smiled. "No ghost. An uprooted tree."

"The ghost turned into a tree. There's ghosts all over this mountain, 'cause it's full of gold. They only let Calico take it. She was belched up from the mountain, too."

"Er . . . this is all news to me," said Irish carefully.

"That's because you only got belched up," Mikie explained. "If you got born like me, you'd know all this stuff." His six-year-old's logic was profound.

And when he saw the tall man's surprised expression he switched tactics with all the innocence of a beggar with sticky palms. "Are you rich like Calico?"

. . . "No," replied Irish, then added. "Is Calico rich?"

"Yeah. Gold rich. She packs it up in mason jars and buries it on the mountain. That's why everybody says she can find gold where God only put a stump. She buries it under 'em."

"I see," Irish said, prone to ignore such a wild tale, but a chip of memory recalled part of his conversation with Phillip Braeswood. *A queer old prospector and his granddaughter*—how was it that he hadn't put it together? A chill rattled his heart. Rich. He had no use for rich women. Belle had cured him of that proclivity. He would never again subject himself to the charity of another, no matter that the label applied had been called love.

"If you ain't rich, then you gotta work. What kind of work do you do?" Mikie asked, full of avid curiosity.

"Scientific," Irish answered, discovering a way to rid himself of this two-and-a-half-foot menace.

"You mean like new math?" the child pressed, very nearly losing interest.

"No. Research, dissecting."

Mikie pondered that for a long moment. "You mean like cuttin' up frogs and such?"

Irish put on his classroom face, stern, professional and no-nonsense. "Not frogs. People."

Mikie swallowed hard, backing away. "No foolin'," he whispered.

Irish hid a smile and raised his eyes, watching Calico come gliding across the room. She moved with seductive, indolent grace, her quicksilver eyes filling with a hunger as she approached. He felt an urgency begin to swell in his loins. Wanting her was an anathema to him, like a poison creeping and piling up in every crevice of his body, and yet, he knew he had to have her.

"You've met Mikie and survived," she said, smiling, and the smile was just for him. "He's the terror of Jobeth's brood." She tapped the child on his shoulder. "Go join Rafe, there's cake and hot cocoa on the table for you."

"More uninvited guests?" Irish queried.

Her brows knitted together in a frown. "Jobeth had an emergency. They're spending the night." The dismay in her voice conveyed itself to Irish. He felt robbed somehow. "Was Mikie bothering you?"

"Educating me on mountain lore. I wasn't born." *Which would solve a lot of my problems,* he thought. "It seems I've been belched up, and you're rich?"

It was as if he were warning her to say no, castigating her in some manner. She hesitated. "Gossip.

These mountains are full of it, like a second crop."

Funny, until this moment, he hadn't credited her with a job or work of any sort. She existed, that was enough. Now it seemed important to know. There was a harsh line around his mouth as he asked, tight lipped, "What do you do when you're not hauling unemployed research scientists from a watery grave?"

She scanned his face, searching for some clue, some indication for his perverseness and found nothing. "I'm a placer miner. I pan and dredge gold from the river."

"An unusual occupation," he replied silkily.

"You sound as though you object to it. It's the only thing I know, and it keeps us fed and clothed and the taxes paid." This simple direct answer seemed to appease him. "Do you mind sharing your bed?"

"With you?"

"I—no." Thoughts of his kisses were still thronging in her mind. "With one of the boys." He shrugged and gave her a small smile of regret.

"Is my bath still on?"

"Yes. You first, then the boys." Aware that his eyes lingered on her, Calico felt her nerves as sharp and ragged as a logger's saw as she went about rolling the old-fashioned hip tub from behind the stove. She filled it with hot water from the stove's reservoir, pulled up a chair and laid out washcloth, towel and soap. Then she spoke to the children. "You two go sit on the sofa and stay there until Irish finishes his bath. And mind, keep your eyes to yourself."

"Aw, we know what men look like," Mikie said. "We're men ourselves."

"Just do as I say."

"Can we look at rocks through your magnifying glass?" Rafe wanted to know.

"There's a box under my desk, pick out a few, and don't break the glass," she replied.

"If we find any with gold in them, can we crush it out?"

"We'll see." She nodded to Irish. "I'll be in my room, give a knock when you're finished." Inertia held Calico against her bedroom door for a moment. Apprehension lurked within her, like a coil about to spring. She was possessed of a secret shame, a stigma, and against this disgrace she had raised a barricade of pride, arrayed a defense of hate. Two powerful emotions so interwoven in the thread of her being that they now threatened to thrust their ugly heads when she no longer wanted to acknowledge their existence.

And if she couldn't control those old feelings, those old turmoils, how, she wondered, was she to manage this newer savage turmoil provoked and ignited by the man who at this very minute was bathing his lean solid body in her tub?

The simple reality—and Calico never turned her back on reality—was that she craved Irish McCaulley, and nothing could blunt the longing that drew her so irresistibly, so inexorably toward him.

The excitement that grew in her was like gold fever. It was that same wrenching expectation she felt when she kneaded mud and rocks in her gold pan. She just knew when she'd worked it down to the auriferous sand, there would be pay dirt, grains of gold, or perhaps a nugget. It was a daring feeling, like stumbling at the edge of a chasm or a deep cave, a feeling that made her heart stop beating, and a tiny shocked laugh escaped from her throat to eclipse the fear.

She loosened the braid and brushed her hair until it gleamed, then pinned it in an entrancing coil atop her head. Unaccustomed to such restraint, vagrant wisps crept down her neck like threads of wild silk.

"Calico...?"

She stopped peering into the faded mirror. "Yes—"

"All clear out here."

She opened the door, their eyes met, each reading the other's message veiled beneath thick lashes and knowing it for what it was. A single question rose in Calico's mind. *Would he know?*

"Your pint-sized houseguests are beginning to droop," Irish said.

Calico herded the youngsters to the tub and was stridently informed that they didn't undress in front of girls. She left them to it and went to sit on the footstool at the hearth, hidden from their view by the sofa. Irish gave her a funny little smile.

"They'll change their minds along about ten or fifteen years from now," he observed dryly.

It wasn't a comment that required an answer. "There's more brandy in the pie safe if you want it."

He did. He needed a sedative, something—anything—to act as a restraint, calm his mind and that certain part of him that was becoming so active, so filled with heat that he was distracted beyond measure. My God! When she'd opened her bedroom door to him, he had very nearly lost his breath. Her hair piled on top of her head like that, emphasizing the slender column of her neck, those lovely hollows where the vein pulsated. Set against her masculine attire, she was like a nubile goddess in disguise. Hell yes, he needed a drink. Clad in pajamas, Rafe and Mikie were ushered onto the back porch by Calico to brush their teeth, after which she directed them to bed.

"I ain't sleeping with no girl," Mikie protested, "And I ain't sleeping with him." He pointed a short stubby finger at Irish.

"We want to sleep together," Rafe said adamantly, his arm protectively about Mikie's shoulder.

"Let them take my bed," Irish volunteered. "I'll bunk down on the sofa."

Calico thought to rail against this, then changed

her mind and led the boys to Christian's bed. They were asleep almost immediately. While Irish meditated in front of the fire, she moved about the kitchen area, finishing the dishes, emptying the tub.

"Can I help you with anything?" He had moved across the room silently in stocking feet. He wore a short terry robe, dark green, and the bottom half of a pair of green-and-white striped pajamas, and where the robe gaped she saw dark hair on his chest curling over the tape that bound his ribs. She remembered how firm his chest had felt to her, how like wiry silk his hair when she'd been driven to touch him.

"You can get that bucket from under the sink and fill the stove reservoir with water," she acknowledged. "You sure pumping won't hurt your chest?"

"I can manage."

She hung damp towels on the line across the back porch, holding her warm flushed face to the chill air for a moment before returning to the kitchen. With Irish's help it took less than ten minutes to put everything to rights and he moved back to the hearth. He fed several chunks of wood into the fire, and while she made up the sofa with quilts and pillows he perused the wall of books.

"You do a lot of reading...."

"Cold winter nights, no television," she murmured. To her, each step he took, the manner in which he drew his fingers down the back of the books seemed deliberate, as if he was pacing himself.

"Aren't you tired?" he asked suddenly. "It's been a long and busy day...taking care of me, cooking, cleaning, and now, taking care of the boys?"

"I'm used to it." In truth, she was saturated with adrenaline, the same way she felt when a storm swooped down on the mountain. Only now the storm was within her, raging with erotic energy. He moved to stand in front of her. The kerosene lantern beside the sofa sputtered and died—out of fuel. Firelight flickered and danced across her face and his.

"I have to kiss you again," he said, his voice thick and husky with emotion. "I've been begging myself not to ...." This he muttered softly into her hair as he slipped an arm about her waist, pulling her close until he felt her soft thrusting breasts vague against his chest, and he cursed silently the tape that bound him.

A sigh escaped Calico's lips and her eyes were heavy lidded with desire. "I want you to—" But his lips closed over hers and there was no more talking, only a keen awareness as nerve endings quivered and gloried in the plundering. His warm moist tongue tasting of brandy thrust into her mouth, and she gave a tiny exploring suck and he groaned. She felt the force of him as it grew hard against her thighs, and her hands circled his neck, her fingers touching him lightly, impetuously while his mouth devoured hers, his tongue a wild erotic being that thrust and thrust. And then he was caressing her earlobes, her eyelids, her throat, but it seemed he could not linger long away from her shapely beckoning mouth, and he found her lips again, nibbling on the lower, tracing the upper until she swayed against his thighs, pressing upon his hardness, inviting him, aching for him, urging him.

The rising spreading warmth inside Calico emanated from a sexual clamor that had long been buried. It could have surfaced with other men, but it had not, for until now she had let none near her. She had found Irish during the storm when she was most vulnerable and it was as though the mountain was giving its blessing. She felt the spirits of her mother and her grandmother, knowing now why their ghostly souls at times seemed so close, so warm. They had been loved. As Irish's hands kneaded her back, then moved lower, his strong fingers moving over her curving hips and pressing her close, she gave herself up to him. A wild low moan escaped her lips, her body trembled and the small movement caused his passion to soar, though it reached heights no greater than her own. And then she felt herself floating free, like a sparrow coasting on a warm windy draft. It took her a moment to realize that his arms had dropped away, his lips had left hers as though he could absorb no more. She raised her lashes to look at him, dazed that he had stopped.

She quivered with leftover sensations that had somehow been lost in the maelstrom and only now were catching up. "Why?" she rasped, her voice etched with unabated wanting. "Why have you stopped?"

He sat on the sofa, taking a long shuddering breath. "You'd better get off to bed...."

Calico's legs wouldn't hold her for another second. She dropped down to sit on the footstool. "I...don't you want me?" she asked in a choked whisper.

He shoved his fingers through his curls and gave a low snicker of sardonic laughter. "Want you? Are you always so direct?"

"Is that so wrong? I want to know."

"Of course I want you!" he exclaimed impatiently. "You think a man acts the way I have if he doesn't want to bed a woman?"

She took a deep breath. "Have you bedded many?"

"Is this an inquisition?" he said stiffly.

"No. I was just wondering...."

She was sucking him in with those eyes. He resisted. "A few other women, one wife."

"Wife?" Calico uttered the word like a long low wail of pain, going so pale only the glow of the fire gave any color to her face.

"Long gone."

It took her a minute to absorb his answer. "Something's wrong with me, then? I'm not sophisticated enough for you?"

He shook his head, amazed. "Calico—I know the human body inside and out—there's nothing wrong with you. Sophistication? You come by it naturally. You are what you are, you haven't been tainted by commercial propaganda...it's wonderfully refreshing."

"Then...why?" Her vanity was closing in on her.

"I could give you a thousand reasons and all would be wrong. Let's just say I have a respect for you that I've never had for another woman." There was a mixture of sadness and sarcasm in his voice.

He knows, she thought. Oh, he knows, he can tell, and that's why he doesn't want me.

He leaned forward and drew a fingertip lightly down her cheek, across her parted lips. "You're a temptress, a beautiful temptress...." Softly whispered words. Calico felt a thrill go through her. No one had ever called her that. "Now, go to bed," *or I'll ravage you right here, this minute, and regret it the rest of my life. I can give you nothing. You deserve more than a taker— and I would take and take and take....*

He lay down on the sofa, pulling the quilts over himself, closing his eyes to blot her out, forcing thoughts away from his lips, his hands that knew every curve still scorching from the feel of her. He crooked an elbow over his eyes. He had longed for his father and it came to nothing; he loved his work and got fired, and now there was this ache in him for Calico and he thought, good things don't come true and bad things don't go away.

He tossed and turned the night away.

Calico didn't sleep at all.

7

IT WAS THAT LAST MINUTE or two before dawn when the sun was still caught behind the mountain and its first golden fingers stretched out to touch Calico as she washed her face and brushed her teeth on the back porch. She had dressed as quietly as she could, donning fitted beige cords, a red-and-white striped oxford shirt, chukka boots, and she had again pinned her hair atop her head. In the privacy of her room she had annointed her body with Anais Anais—lily scented, extravagant, a woman's ploy, a lure, she thought, and one she hoped would work. Then she went into the cabin to begin breakfast; great slices of hickory-cured bacon, creamy grits, eggs from her own chickens. She glanced once at Irish as he lay on the sofa when she went to wake the boys.

Sam, reveling in the freedom and space of the out-of-doors alerted them to Jobeth's arrival before Calico heard the truck straining up the mountain.

"Finish your breakfast," she urged Rafe and Mikie, going to the window to look out and seeing the truck rounding the bend far below. "Your mother's here."

Irish tossed about on the sofa, then sat up, rubbing sleep from his face. "Morning," he said. "Sam stirred up about something?"

She brought him coffee. "My friend, Jobeth. She's come to take the boys to school."

There was a squeal of brakes, steps on the porch and the front door slammed open without a knock.

Judalon Tarrant stood on the threshold, unshaven,

slovenly, hulking, filling the cabin with the smell of
sour sweat and old whiskey. Jail smell. His black eyes
were red rimmed, and his thick lips curved into a
sneer as he picked out Calico and glared at her.

She froze, staring at him horrified.

"Pa!" the boys chorused in unison, sounding slightly dismayed.

And Calico was thinking, *It's all a nightmare, I
haven't gotten up yet.* Her eyes darted to Judalon, to
Irish, back to Judalon. A savage anger shot through
her, building, building until she was incoherent with
rage, yet driven in her anger to speak.

"You had no right to walk in here without knocking, Judalon! No right even to be on this mountain."

"I come to git my boys. You trying to keep me from
them?"

Her hands were so tightly clenched into fists they
were white, bloodless. "No, but you get out of my
house! Wait on the porch."

"You ain't big enough to make me. You can't make
me do nothin'." His bloodshot eyes gleamed with re-
membrance. "We settled that once before, ain't we?"

Calico suddenly felt faint. Irish stood up, watching
her, then his gaze swung to the smelly hulking giant
on the threshold. There was an undercurrent of tension, and something more. His first impulse was to
back Calico, and he moved across the room, ostensi-
bly to refill his coffee cup.

Judalon turned a venomous look on Calico. "Got
you a fella, huh? Well—he ain't gittin' nothin' special."

Irish bristled. "Look, Mister, the lady asked you to
wait on the porch." There was something in the way
he said it, the soft menace, the lack of fear that made
Judalon take note, size him up. He took a step backward.

"I ain't lookin' for no trouble. I just ain't had my

coffee yet, been a miserable night. If I could have a cup...?" he whined, changing tack.

Irish poured a cup over Calico's silent protest. Judalon took it from him without a thank-you. "Rafe, Mikie, you two git on out to the truck." He turned to Calico as the boys edged around him, saucer eyed. "I brung you a message from Jeb if you want it."

Tight lipped, Calico refused to be drawn into conversation with Judalon, staring at him with stark indignation. Then she discovered Irish looking at her in a strange way, and she had the feeling he was appraising her, looking inside her and there were things there that she didn't want him to see. She spoke to Judalon, harboring the hate, the anger, storing it deep inside where it wouldn't show. "What's the message?" *No use... no use.* She still sounded malevolent.

"Your grampa's doing fine."

She choked out a thank-you.

Finally, finally, he left, driving off down the clay-packed road. Calico seemed to shrivel. Irish turned from the window and walked over to her and traced her face gently with his fingers. Then he led her to a chair, sat her down and made their breakfast. He put a plate in front of her.

"I'm not hungry."

"One bite," he urged, unsure exactly what the problem was, only positive he must bring her back from whatever depth of hell she had just visited.

She looked down at the plate, unseeing, then back at him, her gray eyes huge, somber, falling somewhere into an inner sanctum he was not allowed to touch. "Do you like me?" she asked in a voice barely audible.

"Very much," he assured her.

She got up from the table and locked the doors, then she stood in front of the fireplace and began to unbutton her blouse. Her eyes never left his face. "How much?"

Irish put down his fork. His heart beat like a becrazed dervish, and he told himself; *Just this once, and then I've got to get off this mountain.* The blouse slipped slowly from her shoulders, over her breasts until they burst free, waiting for his touch, taunting him. "This is crazy," he murmured thickly, not understanding the compulsion that impelled him across the room to her. It was foreign to his thinking, there was nothing scientific about it, nothing logical.

When his hands moved to cup her breasts gently, Calico knew in that moment that she would have to live with her shame forever. Bury it in some dark recess of her mind and let it lie. She smiled into his green eyes as if irrevocably those eyes and the life behind them were her own. "This is destiny," she said in a choked whisper.

And then his mouth was hovering near hers, saying her name over and over, a litany, like a prayer, like a man lost begging for succor, and in a single fluid motion he swept her into his arms and took her to her bed.

He threw off his robe, his pajamas, and the sight of him—strong, hard, aroused, evoked emotions in her that were terrifying in their intensity, far more electric than her dreams. He joined her on the bed, the soft down coverlets a cushion, a sanctuary, and began stroking her with his lean competent fingers, featherlight touches—too much and not enough. His lips were everywhere, igniting the flame, his hands trailing after them, urgent probing, causing the flame to rage out of control, pursuing an incredible rapture. She moved back slightly and began to caress his thighs, his stomach, his chest, and her lips sought out his, opening to him, beckoning him in.

"You're pushing me past all endurance," she whis-

pered, begging him to enter her, and that first inde-
scribable thrust was a sensation she would remember
for the rest of her life. Her hips moved hesitantly until
the rhythm was a ritual untaught, instinctive, pounding; his flesh searing hers, her long legs, silky against
his muscular ones. She shook with a tiny series of
wondrous explosions and Irish begged her not to
move, but her slender back arched against him and he
drove into her exploding and all that he was—the
past, the present, the future—flowed from him, filling
her, and he expelled a deep guttural moan of pleasure
that was unleashed from his very marrow.

"I WAS AWFUL," whispered Calico as they untangled
arms and legs.

Irish leaned on an elbow, looking at her while he
touched her face gently with his fingers. "You were
wonderful. I've never made love to an enchantress
before," he told her, hearing his own voice, but not
feeling his tongue shape the words.

"I've never really been loved at all," she answered.
Her silvery gray eyes were filled with candor as she
inspected him in return, all the while marveling that
their bodies could come together as they had and that
still she had this urge of wanton desire she couldn't
stop from building. "I want to do that again," she
murmured. "I *know* I was just awful the first time."

"You weren't," he assured her. "Let me have some
time to recover. I'm injured, remember?" He moved
away and lay on his back, closing his eyes, while a
tiny little smile hovered on his lips.

"It hurts you to do this?" she asked, watching his
face as she trailed her fingertips tantalizingly down
his flat belly close to his tumescent flesh. It was powerful, majestic, lusting, making her grow warm and
moist again. The hollow feeling that was engulfing
her demanded surfeit.

"No, no, it doesn't hurt a bit," he said, barely audible. When her fingers crept closer Irish gave a guttural sigh and with his hands, guided her hips over his and Calico learned new pleasures—fiery, undulating, magnificent carnal pleasures that made her feel like she was travelling from mountaintop to mountaintop without ever once setting foot in the valleys.

"NOW I'M HUNGRY," Calico admitted with flagrant abandon as she and Irish sat on the porch steps side by side, balancing plates on their knees. A sun-warmed wind blowing gently down the sluice sent autumn-colored leaves dancing across the yard. Calico's gaze followed a leaf until it tumbled into the river. Nearer the steps Sam was devouring their earlier, now congealed breakfast, for him, a feast. Her hens loitered at his flank waiting for a chance to snatch a tidbit from his bowl.

"Thank God it's for food," Irish muttered, teasing her, thinking that if he had to walk more than a dozen steps his legs wouldn't be able to support him.

"I've never talked about sex before," she told him, watching him out of the corner of her eye.

He felt a little telltale quiver. "Let's not start now. I need refueling." He stabbed at the golden yoke on his plate.

"Are you really that weak?"

"Everything about me is weak."

"Oh." She didn't feel the least bit weak. Just the opposite. She was reveling in the afterglow of sex; she felt energized without suffering her old nemesis, restlessness. "Is it your age?" she asked in all innocence. "I've always heard—"

His ego was lanced and he nearly choked on a biscuit. "Age has nothing to do with it. I'm only forty-two, anyway. I have a few good years left yet."

"I'm glad to hear that," she remarked snidely, and

after the look he bestowed on her thought she'd better
hold her tongue for a while. She didn't want him
choking to death after she'd saved him from drowning and seen him back to health.

It was true that she had never discussed sex, but she
didn't see how anyone could have described it anyway, at least, not so a person could understand it. All
those wonderful sensations bombarding her...she
wouldn't have believed it possible, not after—She deflected that thought.

She had never considered herself an old maid, but
now she felt pity for those few she did know, and the
several widows, too. Oh, how they must suffer. She
crumbled a biscuit and tossed it to the chickens, using
the action to cast a surreptitious glance at Irish. He
was attractive in profile, his nose strong, his chin
firm, his eyes like true malachite with ebony flecks,
and in her mind's eye she was seeing him naked,
making love to her and she wondered why any
woman would leave him—would let him go. If he belonged to her, *really belonged*, she'd never let him out
of her sight. This idea caused her to have a dreadful
curiosity that she couldn't contain. "What happened
between you and your wife?" she asked softly.

His expression changed from one of contentment to
one of almost brutal savagery. Calico recoiled as if
slapped. "Just like that. You think you have the right
to ask?"

"I...yes. Don't I...after this morning?" She was
overwhelmed with a sense of dread, fearing his answer.

"The past is the past," he stated. There was no
change in the level of his voice, but it had taken on a
dangerous edge. "Belle wasn't for me. She's a woman
any man can have."

Calico's throat constricted, but she couldn't leave it

alone. "You mean she's slept with another man, and that's the reason you don't want her?" She felt very, very cold.

"Exactly. I was raised in an orphanage on seconds and hand-me-downs. I don't want a secondhand wife. Now can you lay off?"

"Yes," she said stiffly.

Whatever it was between them, she didn't want it to end this way. She didn't want to erase that warm afterglow so soon, and above all she didn't want to think of herself as a second, but it hung in her mind like a worrisome rock caught in her shoe. The subject needed changing. She waited until they were drinking refills of coffee and the angry glint had faded from his eyes.

"I was born right here on the mountain. Up there." She pointed to a shadowy outcrop of rock covered with cudzu vines that hid an imperceptible slit in the face of the mountain. "There's an entrance to an old gold mine. You can't see it unless you know where to look."

"You were born in a gold mine?"

His tone held only interest, nothing of anger. Calico sighed inwardly. "On that grass slick beside it. My daddy was exploring the mine while my mother stood outside paying out the rope that was his lifeline to the surface when the shaft collapsed. My mother tried to dig him out, skinning her fingers to the bone, but she couldn't, and it was time for me, and she didn't want to leave my daddy, so she laid down right there and had me. Jeb found us. He had come up to tell them grampa was coming home. He found me between my mother's legs. She was dead, and my daddy is still buried up there. Grampa put a cross next to my mother's on the scree because it seemed a fitting thing to do."

"A cenotaph," Irish said, glancing up at the leaning white cross erected to honor a man crushed beneath tons of mountain. He shuddered. "That's nice," he murmured.

Calico gave him a withering look. "To be dead?"

"I didn't mean that. To know your heritage, where you came from, to know your people." It was a thing for which he had longed his entire life, and he was coming dangerously close to revealing the abyss he kept locked beneath his pride. He was overcome with a sudden urge to leave, to get off this mountain, to get away from her.

"Wanting to see, wanting to know," Calico remarked, catching the wistful slant in the slight hoarseness of his answer. She gave him an appraising glance. "Maybe you're an incurable romantic."

He laughed. "I've been called many a thing, but never that. Could be you see something in me that no one else ever has." He didn't know it, but right then he had opened the door and let her in.

Her face reflected a mixture of truth and uncertainty. "I wanted to see my daddy once. I found another entrance to the mine and crawled down it, but the mountain began to rumble and I backed out of there in a hurry. Scared me."

"You? Scared?" A hint of a lazy smile tilted the corners of his mouth. "What's it like, going down in one of those old shafts?"

"Well, in the first place, sometimes you don't go down, you angle up, but it's always dark, cold too, after a while, and wet if its close to a river or a stream." She turned to Irish. "Would you like for me to take you exploring or teach you to pan for gold?"

He declined. "Another time, perhaps."

"Your head hurts?" she queried anxiously. "Your leg? Your chest?"

He shook his head. "I need to think about returning

to Atlanta. When do you think you'll know about your grandfather?''

She pretended not to hear. "Why is it you don't have a job?''

"I was fired,'' he replied, dipping into his well of pride in order to utter the words. "I did a very dumb thing. I ignored the rumors I'd heard about our department chairman. Some said he was an insecure man, others that he was afraid for his job and that nobody in his department ever got tenure because Vincent was afraid that if any scientist got tenure they'd be primed to step into his shoes.''

"Vincent?'' Calico's hand went to her neck, remembering Irish bolting upright in bed, grabbing her.

Irish reached over and stroked her neck gently. "I'm sorry about doing that,'' he said softly. "I guess it was still fresh in my mind...six wasted years at Albert Bateman.''

"Albert Bateman? Why, that's where my grampa took his training! His certificate's in our Bible.''

"Your grandfather's a physician?''

"He used to be. He doesn't practice and hasn't for fifty years.''

"Why not? That's a lot of education to let go to waste.''

"The state took his licence away. He killed a man he thought deserved to die and spent twenty years in prison.''

"That does go a bit against the Hippocratic oath,'' Irish observed, a tinge of sarcasm in his voice.

She stiffened. "It didn't have anything to do with medicine.'' The sound of a motor saved any further possible argument and they both stood up. Calico recognized the light blue pickup as it swerved around the bend. "It's my cousin, Jebediah Bascomb,'' she informed Irish. "He must have—''

Her grampa was in the truck.

Calico left Irish standing in deep shadow on the porch and hurried to the passenger side of the pickup as it slammed to a halt in the yard.

"Grampa! Jeb! Grampa, why aren't you in the hospital?" she demanded. He looked old and worn, his skin so parchment transparent the veins showed through. He'd always seemed old to her, but never aging; gray headed, gray bearded, yet now there was a sunken look about him. It frightened her.

Her grampa gazed at her through watery blue eyes and tried out a thin wavering smile. "I heard the mountain calling. Anyway, I don't like hospitals and, besides, I got thirsty."

"Mountain calling!" Snorted Calico, leaning forward, smelling the fresh whiskey on Christian's breath. Her eyes flashed angrily. "Grampa, you're drunk. You never talk crazy like this unless—"

"Having a mission in life isn't crazy. My mission is on Talking Rock. I know it."

Calico's heart sank and she looked pleadingly at Jebediah who shrugged as eloquently as an eighty-year-old can. "Weren't nothing I could do. Doc Willis didn't want to turn him loose, but Christian told the hospital he wouldn't pay 'em for a minute past nine o'clock this morning...."

"So he just walked out?" she exclaimed. "You crazy old man!"

"I hobbled out. Got me a pair of crutches." He fumbled for the handle, trying to open the door. Calico leaned against it. With her grampa home, there would be no excuse, no reason she could hold Irish here.

"No Grampa," she said firmly. "You're still sick, your foot—" She cajoled, wheedled, but her grandfather was in no mood for argument, merely sitting there opposing her with a stolid inertia, and every now and then taking a swig from a jar he held between his knees.

Calico talked until she was hoarse. "Jeb, please, you convince him," she pleaded finally, but in the end she knew it was futile and jerked the door open. Christian's ankle and foot were in a cast. It looked odd because where his toes should have been there were only pads of gauze. Refusing her help, Christian settled himself on his crutches. Calico turned toward the cabin. Irish was leaning casually against the old log railing.

"Grampa, there's someone here I want you to meet. The man I pulled from the river."

"I've heard about him. He still here?" He was watching carefully where he put the crutch pegs, avoiding loose rock and gravel that would imperil his progress.

"On the porch. I'll introduce you."

At the bottom of the steps, Christian looked up as Irish moved from the shadows into the sunlight, an expectant expression on his face. Long and lean, his shaggy features were sharply delineated as he stepped forward and his green eyes seemed to glitter.

Christian paused, staring fixedly at Irish. His mind was fogged with whiskey, with pain; it was the eyes that struck him. He'd seen eyes like those only once before. Even in his drink-befuddled brain, he knew— *he knew*! But it couldn't be. He didn't want it to be. Fate was luring him into his past, a cruel painful past he'd spent years disremembering. This couldn't be what the waiting was all about, but the knowing jolted awake a long dormant chip of recollection. It was an explosive predestined moment for him. His eyes bulged, blood ran in a terrifying pace to his heart, which could not pump it through. "Parsons," he gurgled, and pitched forward drunkenly, staggering up one step, losing his balance, the crutches flying. Calico screamed and snatched at his shirt collar and kept his head from slamming into the steps as he collapsed.

"What'd he say? My God!" she cried in panic.

"It's the drink," said Irish. "He's just passed out."

"No, he's fainted. Look at his face! It's turning blue!"

Irish moved swiftly, lifting the old man onto the porch. "Let me have a look," he said, examining Christian quickly, skillfully, flipping back an eyelid, taking his pulse, finding it slowing...slowing...slowing.

"What's wrong?" The words were wrung from Calico. She knelt beside her grandfather, trembling as color drained from her cheeks.

"I...it looks like a heart attack and it doesn't," Irish replied uncertainly. "Whatever it is, he needs medical attention and fast."

The next several hours were a blur. A pallet was constructed on the bed of Jebediah's truck, and Christian was laid there with Irish watching over him as they sped into Gainsville. Calico followed in her truck. At the hospital Doc Willis stabilized Christian, then pulled Calico aside. "This is beyond me. I've made arrangements to have him admitted to Emory in Atlanta. I'm sending him by ambulance, now."

"What's wrong with him?" she pleaded, realizing it was serious but not wanting to believe it was so bad that Doc Willis couldn't explain it.

"I'm telling you, it's beyond my expertise," he replied with a small exasperated sigh. "I'm just a country practitioner. There's no heart damage. It's shock of some sort. Look, it's going to be expensive...."

"I'll sell some gold."

Doc Willis smiled. "Now I know you're upset. For all your reputation, I've never known you to admit you own any."

Her great gray eyes were somber. "People take." Her voice was unemphatic, flat, and Doc Willis wished he'd saved the comment for another time.

There was a flurry of activity as Christian was

loaded into the ambulance, and Irish approached the driver, shook his hand, then moved to join Calico on the emergency-room dock. "I'm hitching a ride back to Atlanta." He squeezed her shoulder, and his touch made her skin burn. "I'll be back to get Sam, my car and other things...."

"But—" She couldn't keep him. Her thick fringe of lashes hid the panic in her eyes. He knew of her shame then, he'd guessed, he'd only made love to her because she'd thrown herself at him, begged. Everything inside was crumbling, falling, crashing like an old mine unable to sustain its walls, its roof sagging. She couldn't answer. She was too full of conflicting and confusing thoughts. She watched the ambulance speed away, its siren wailing like she wanted to wail.

"Calico...?" Doc Willis touched her elbow. She looked at him, her face bereft of expression. "I know you're worried," he said gently, "but take the time to go home, see to things and pack a few items. There's a motel near Emory. If it's what I think, they'll need you."

EMORY UNIVERSITY HOSPITAL was a vast complex of buildings filled with a bewildering array of corridors, nurses' stations, operating rooms, cafeterias, and the staff seemed busily intent on their jobs. Nurses were overworked and brusque, doctors impersonal. Calico sat with Christian from eight in the morning until eight at night. Sometimes he knew her and sometimes not. When he was himself he talked to her, pleading for her to take him home. When he wasn't, and that could be the very next instant, he mumbled only to himself.

She went back to her room at the Ramada Inn each night exhausted—from doing nothing. The food in the hospital cafeteria was tasteless and she ate just enough to curb her appetite. She bathed, crawled between sheets—on the hardest mattress she'd ever slept on—and passed the night reliving every moment she'd spent with Irish McCaulley. His waking, his sleeping, his lovemaking. She knew the feel of his lips, his hands, the length of his long sinewy legs next to hers. By the end of the first week in Atlanta she was in no fit state and could easily have joined Christian as a patient in the hospital, but no one paid her any mind.

Every morning a group of interns and residents led by a chief of surgery, a chief of psychiatry or a chief of something came racing through the wing in which Christian was lodged. They crowded into his small room, ignoring her as though she were some manne- quin.

Today was no different. The group of fifteen crashed into the room surrounding Christian's bed.

"Eighty-two years old," droned the chief of the day, "Classic case of senility...."

Standing in a far corner to stay out of their way, Calico overheard and could abide no more. She pushed through the white-jacketed staffers. "No!" she cried. "He's not senile. This came on him sud- den." Her eyes smoldered with anger. "And...and, you have no right to sweep in here every morning pointing to my grandfather like he's nothing more than a specimen under glass! He has a name—Chris- tian Jones."

The chief of psychiatry, a tall stately looking man, white headed, brown-eyed, stared at Calico as though he were God and she had broken the eleventh com- mandment: Thou shalt not interrupt.

The silence was deafening.

"Sudden?" One of the residents pushed forward, courageous in the vacuum of silence. He had longish hair, wore faded Levis and a threadbare shirt beneath his white smock. "Dr. Marcavitch—may I?" There was no servility in his tone.

"By all means," Dr. Marcavitch drawled, animosity filtering through his voice.

"I've seen this look on faces before."

"Ah, so we're making diagnoses based on the expression a patient wears these days, are we?" remarked the chief scathingly. "Perhaps, Bass, you'd do better joining a Gypsy caravan, telling fortunes."

The man called Bass, older than the other residents, held his ground and said quietly. "If this man had been plucked from a war zone, I'd diagnose him as shell-shocked."

Dr. Marcavitch sneered. "Obviously this old man has not been to war, Bass."

"Perhaps a war of his own making—sir," Bass said, adding the respectful salutation with an overlay of violence and in a manner that pointed up the older doctor's lack of civility.

Dr. Marcavitch attempted to stare down the resident and failed. "All right, Bass, he's yours, as of this minute. Cure him." He spun on his heel and left the room. There was a nervous rustling, a shuffling of feet as the others looked at Bass, carefully hiding their sympathy as they followed their white-haired chief. Bass remained behind and smiled self-consciously at Calico.

"Looks like I burned that one."

They eyed one another for a moment, each taking the other's measure. Calico decided she liked him. "What made you say that about my grandfather? Are you a real doctor?"

He laughed. "You bet I am," he answered with an undertone of force. "This is my last year of residency, then I'm on my own. Now, I don't think I'm too far out on a limb when I say something scared your... Christian. How about having a cup of coffee with me in the cafeteria? I hate talking about patients in front of them, whether they're aware of me or not."

Calico despised the cafeteria coffee, but agreed. Jerry Bass was the first friendly face she'd encountered since she and Christian had arrived. But she protested his thinking Christian was filled with fear. She related the events on Talking Rock.

"You mean Christian looked at this perfect stranger, a man he'd never seen before and just collapsed? Didn't he say anything?"

"He said parson."

"Parson? Like a preacher? Has he had any dealings with a preacher—good, bad or indifferent? I'm talking about a situation that might have dramatic overtones."

"He killed one, if that's what you mean."

Jerry Bass's beard-shadowed jaw gaped, then remembering doctors were never shocked, he clamped his mouth into a tight line. "This stranger, did he look like the preacher?"

Calico shrugged. "I don't know, it happened long before I was born, fifty years ago, then grampa spent twenty years in prison."

Bass rubbed his hands over his face, rubbing out sleeplessness, trying to rub in a clue. The girl across the Formica table fascinated him, he couldn't seem to tear his eyes away from her face. "Well, I'll tell you Calico—is it okay if I call you Calico? Your grampa intrigues me. He's spooked, if you don't mind me using a Viet Nam term, and we've got to find out what spooked him—get him to deal with it, and then we'll see."

"Sometimes he's himself—I mean he knows me—I tell the nurses, but—"

"Yeah, I know. That's a good sign." He was watching her mouth as it shaped words. "I know we like to think of ourselves as motivated by noble deeds, but the fact is we're all driven by lust or greed or power or pride. Something about this stranger you mentioned has triggered a memory, one Christian doesn't like, or maybe he does want to remember and can't. What do you know about the preacher he killed?"

Calico shook her head. "Nothing. He never told me. No one talks about it. I've never asked." She paused a heartbeat, taking a deep breath. "Is there anything else wrong with my grandfather? I know his ankle's broken and his toes are...." Her mouth went dry, remembering herself finding him, remembering the awful thing she had had to do.

"He's as fit a man physically for his age as I've ever seen, considering what he's been through." Dr. Jerry Bass found himself staring at Calico, the strange quality of her features, as though something were stored there just beneath the surface. The man in him, not the physician, wanted to pull it out, examine it, caress it. His hand lifted, reaching out to touch her. He caught himself just in time. "I'd like to keep Christian under observation, talk to him, see if I can get through the steel wall he's thrown up."

A skepticism flared in Calico's eyes. "You'll never do it. When he's drunk he's always carrying on about his mission—whatever that might be—I've never paid him much mind about that. He says the mountain's calling him. Now he's confused and I didn't like seeing him confused. I guess what I'm trying to tell you is that even when he carries on about his mission he seems so...so confident that he has one."

"It may be part of his problem, of what's bothering him. His mission may be the base of that wall he's built around himself. I'd like to find out."

Calico glanced out over the cafeteria, over the white-and-green-clad nurses and doctors, at a porter mopping up a spill. This wasn't the place for grandpa—it was too sterile, too unfriendly. She was mildly surprised to find that the mountain was calling her back, too.

"I'm taking grandpa home."

"No! You can't. He needs help."

A kind of superhuman intensity leaped from Jerry Bass to Calico, making her wonder if she was doing the right thing. Dr. Bass might help grandpa, but in grandpa's lucid moments he wanted to go home.

She was torn and a silence hung between them. "I think you'll be wasting your time, but if you want to pick his brain you'll have to come to Talking Rock."

Jerry Bass drew his hand across his mouth to hide the relieved sigh that escaped his lips. It was more than he had hoped for. "Give me the directions then, and I'll help you get your grandfather checked out."

Calico extended her hand to him. "Thank you."

8

IRISH KNEW EVERY SINGLE INCH of the human body, knew how each part worked, its use, the incredible array of human organs and where they went and how they functioned, yet he couldn't describe exactly where the strange darts of activity he felt were emanating from. But he knew exactly which part of his anatomy they were affecting with maddening regularity, embarrassing regularity. No matter what he did, with whom he was talking, or where he happened to be, he could not remove the vision of Calico standing before her hearth disrobing, and he kept remembering himself between her lovely ivory-skinned thighs.

Forty-two year-old men did not go about becoming infatuated. Other men, perhaps, but not him. Then why the hell did he seem to have the attention span of a one-celled animal that did the same thing over and over? He slammed the suitcase he'd been packing closed and discovered it overfull. He jerked it open, tossed out a dozen pairs of socks and four pairs of slacks.

See, he told himself. Thinking of Calico made him raw inside. If only he could rid himself of this wanting. A drink. He needed a drink, a stiff one. The doorbell peeled insistently, grating on his nerves.

He didn't want company. Reluctantly he went to the door.

"Who is it?"

"Phillip. Ginny said you wanted us to take care of Sam while you're in Kansas City."

Irish opened the door. "I'll be back day after tomorrow. You're sure it's no trouble?"

Phillip watched Irish move about the apartment like an animal on a leash. "No trouble at all. He seems like a different dog after Talking Rock. How's your head?"

"Stitches are out, tape's off. I'm like a new man."

Phillip was thinking Irish displayed none of his usual clipped preciseness. He appeared mellow. No—dazed was more like it. He watched Irish wander over to the patio door and stare out lost in thought. "Hope you have good luck on your job interview in Kansas City. K.U. Med Center, didn't you say?"

No response. Phillip cocked an eyebrow.

"Say, Irish," he added, "you're still going to sell me your apartment, right?"

"Sure."

Thoughtfully Phillip went into the kitchen and made two drinks. Bourbon and soda for himself and bourbon spiked with a full teaspoon of bitters. Irish accepted the drink absently, and Phillip sat down, waiting. The bump Irish had taken on his head had really done the man in, he thought.

After a long few minutes, Irish took a sip of his drink and gagged. "Yuk!" He spun on his heel, his face wild, then he saw Phillip and surprise registered.

"You just agreed to sell me your apartment," Phillip said, grinning.

"Like hell!"

"You said yes, my friend," Phillip assured him, still grinning. "Are you sure you're all right?"

"Positive, I've just so much on my mind."

"I'd like to add to that, if you can absorb it," Phillip said, his tone businesslike. "Something you said piqued my interest."

"Nothing I said could pique your interest," retorted Irish. "You only get excited about dollar signs."

"That's the truth." Phillip gave his lazy grin. "This is about dollars."

"You've got the bull by the wrong end, Phillip."

"Will you let me string a few sentences together without interruption for crying out loud? About this lab of yours, suppose you discovered some cure, some medicine, or something of use to the industrial market. Who owns it?"

"I would, but you're talking like heaven is only a door you have to knock on to gain entrance."

"But—what would you own," Phillip persisted.

"A patent."

"And patents are worth money, right? If—suppose you had an investor or several investors to finance a laboratory. Would the investor share ownership of the patent?"

Irish felt just a tiny twinge of excitement, gut level. "You're talking about a huge amount of money, Phillip. Two hundred thousand dollars to equip a lab, not including the building, test animals, an assistant. And a scientist could work his entire life and never make any grand discoveries." It was a warning. "Where would that leave you?"

"With a bountiful and acceptable tax write-off against my earnings, which are considerable. You haven't answered my question. Would the investor share ownership of the patent?"

"Depends," Irish said.

"On what?" Phillip gazed at him over the rim of his drink.

"Me."

"Ahhhh," Phillip said and grinned. He leaned back on the rattan sofa and studied Irish. "A man of your stature in the medical community wouldn't have any trouble being awarded grants, would he?"

Irish was scared to breathe. "Not unless I'm up against a Nobel prize winner—at least not so far."

"Still think you want to make that trip to Kansas City?" Phillip asked with a sly smile.

"Yes, it'll give me time to think."

Phillip heaved himself up off the sofa and scooped up Sam. "Well, I'll take your pooch on up to Ginny and Sarah. You'll be back day after tomorrow?" Irish nodded. "Come on upstairs then. We're having a few friends over, people you might like to meet. About seven." Phillip paused at the foot of the stairs in the entrance foyer. "Oh, I forgot to mention—are you and Belle finished?"

"Irrevocably," Irish replied, feeling his stomach go sour. "Why? What has she to do with this?"

"Not a thing." She called Ginny from Boston. I guess bad news travels fast. She knew you were out of work."

ALBERT BATEMAN SCHOOL OF MEDICINE was run under the dual chairmanship of two administrators. One man oversaw the hospital complex, the other ruled the medical school. Between them the two powerful men controlled the unit as a whole.

Mary Lou was just emerging from the powder room when she spotted the joint chief, medical, stepping from the elevator at the end of the corridor. He was headed her way and he looked happy. She hurried to her office and without knocking thrust her head into the office of her boss, Gerald Vincent. He looked up, growling at being disturbed.

"Put on your happy face, Gerald," Mary Lou drawled. "Gustav Brown is headed this way." She popped back to her desk and was typing away industriously when the portly man entered the department chairman's office.

Gustav Brown was obese, effete and silky. He bathed with lavender soap, wore custom-tailored suits and had a mind like a steel trap. He liked to think of himself as a Southern gentleman of the old school, preferred the title mister to doctor and allowed his staff to run their departments as they saw fit. He maintained a hands-off policy as long as all— and he meant all—that they did reflected on the acclaim and glorious image of Bateman. Bateman had graduated more physicians who later won the Nobel prize or the Albert and Mary Laskey award than any other medical college in the United States. His only regret to date was that no staff member, no professor or doctor on his payroll, had yet to be nominated for either prize. But Gustav felt they were close.

Mary Lou buzzed Gerald and waved Gustav into the inner office with her most magnificent smile. Gustav did not miss the fact that all that was typed across the paper in the typewriter was, "Now is the time for all good men to come to the aid of their country." *Come to the aid of Bateman,* he thought, and smiled graciously.

Gerald Vincent came to his feet. "Gustav, what brings the great man to our humble office?"

"Humble?" Gustav smiled warmly. "Your desk is bigger than mine, your carpet thicker and certainly your sculpture is far more exquisite." He passed his fingertips over the Lladro. "I heard the good news about McCaulley. I just thought I'd pop in to congratulate you."

Gerald cocked an eyebrow. "You approve then?" he queried, surprised.

"Approve! For God's sake, Gerald, its laudatory!"

The department chairman beamed and leaned forward conspiratorially as Gustav lowered his vast bulk into the damask chair. "To tell you the truth," said Gerald in a satisfied tone, "I've been trying to get rid of him for the past two years."

"Rid? Gerald, what the hell are you talking about?"

"Why—I fired Irish McCaul—"

Gustav shot out of the chair. "You what!" He was a huge man, and his voice was correspondingly loud. His shout was heard along the outer corridors. His face empurpled and a vein throbbed dangerously in his temple. "You idiot! You've fired the one man in this school with the talent and drive to—" Gustav saw his dream, his most fervent wish for Bateman, dissolve like some wisp of smoke on a windy day. "McCaulley's just been awarded the Potamkin Prize for the work he did last year on Alzheimer's disease! Haven't you opened your mail this morning? We need men like him to bring in grants...money..." He tossed his arms about. "You know what money is, don't you?" he sneered. "It furnished this office! We can't stay afloat without grants—have you bothered to tote up the dollar value McCaulley's brought into the school in grants over the past six years? Millions—"

"We can accept the award for him," Vincent said in a small voice.

"It's personal, goes with a $25,000 cash award." Gustav's voice was steely. "Listen to me, Gerald. You've been hiding behind that desk and your fluffed-up chair for fifteen years—now you get your ass out there and you get McCaulley back in this school, and if you don't or you can't," his voice boomed ominously, "you're out!"

9

WATCHING CHRISTIAN, Calico wondered if she'd made a terrible mistake. She thought about all the care he would have gotten if she'd kept him in Emory. She lived in a constant state of panic. He was having longer and longer periods of lucidity, so that she could leave him at the cabin, but she was frightened to go farther than calling distance, and she never went where the cabin would be out of her sight. She worried about the moments he had when he seemed so lost, feared that he would wander over the mountain and fall into one of the cuts or an old mining shaft.

Yet, she had to work. She had to replace the gold she'd sold, the money spent at Emory and the motel in Atlanta. The tree that had carried Irish McCaulley down the sluice to the elbow in the river had gouged out a deep groove down to the bedrock. It was filling with gold and it was this groove that she worked each day with an old dredge. Sometimes Christian hobbled down to the river on his crutches and sat there, watching, encouraging, but the trip back up the incline drained him. She pretended not to notice.

Jebediah and Winnie came as often as they could to sit with Christian and this freed her for a few hours. Today, Jeb was alone, Winnie had her quilting circle. Calico stirred the pot of creamy potato soup simmering in the stove well. ''Jeb, there's corn bread in the warmer and the soup's ready. You and grampa eat

something before you empty out that jar of brandy."
She walked over to Christian and squeezed his
shoulder.

"I'm going to scout the river today," she told him.
"Follow it up to the cave, find some likely holes to
pan. You take care of yourself while I'm gone."

"Get off with you, Calico. Stop fluttering about,
gives me the shudders," Christian muttered in his
gravelly voice. She left him at the sofa and lifted the
gun belt off the back door, draping it around her neck.
Jebediah watched her with growing alarm.

"What do you need that for?" he asked.

"Dogs, bears, snakes." *Trespassers*, she thought.

"The weather's turning off cool. You're not likely to
run up on any."

"When the sun's out, no matter how cool, snakes
crawl, Jeb. You know that. I'll be in the rocks."

The old men followed Calico to the porch and
watched her take off across the mountain.

"Something's pestering her, sure." Christian said
when she was out of hearing range.

"Winnie says she's took with that man she hauled
out of the river," Jeb enlightened him.

Christian folded himself onto the old sofa, relishing
the warmth of the sun. The broody hen had hatched
her chicks and now made her nest beneath the porch
steps. "I wish I'd a chance to meet him," he said,
missing the troubled look on Jebediah's face.

"He was here when I brought you home from the
hospital that first time."

"Funny. I don't recall it," Christian told him. He
stared at the cast on his ankle. "What do you suppose
would be best to whittle out me some toes? Pine or
poplar?"

"Neither," Jebediah answered. "Both too light,
you're going to need something with weight, hold
your balance."

Christian gave a sly grin. "Hollow it out. I got me some gold stashed away. We'll use it for ballast."

THE RIVER WAS BACK TO NORMAL, rushing as always down the mountain, but clear, so that she could see the fish, the rockstrewn bottom. Calico strode beside it, following the groove left by the tree wherever it had touched down. She spent no time at the sluice where the beavers had repaired their dam and lodge. Everything that had ever happened to her at that spot had been bad, turning her life into one of lingering loneliness. She knew gold was drifting down to the foot of the dam and that one day she'd have to explore it. But not today.

She felt strange, anxious, the longing in her keeping her on edge. She missed Irish McCaulley more than she cared to admit. She skirted Phillip Braeswood's cabin. The sports car was gone, had been when she returned with Christian from Atlanta; his clothes, his dog, too. But on the cabin door there still fluttered the tattered note left by Irish McCaulley. A man apart, she thought, a man who leaves sign—for his unknown parent.

She strolled along the river's edge. Right here, she surmised, was where Irish had been standing when jerked into the flooded river. She glanced at the washout across the expanse of water, then at her feet. Her breath caught in her throat.

There, ground into wet mudlike red clay was a wallet. His wallet, she was positive even before she stooped to retrieve it, open it and inspect it. And in that instant she decided to go to Atlanta to call on Irish McCaulley. Christian could stay with Jeb and Winnie.

She moved away from the river's edge to sit on a boulder and let the compulsion for Irish wash over her. It manifested itself in the warmth in her thighs, the aching in her nipples. She wanted to see him, smell him, touch him. Her breath came in small short bursts, her lips parted as she became submerged in erotic reverie. All around her was the mountain, the soft susurrus of the river as it met a boulder midstream, murmured against it and moved on, the gentle rustling of autumn-colored leaves brushed by the wind—earth music for the rhythm of lovemaking in her mind's eye.

A harsh note suddenly shattered her vision and her gaze swept the landscape through narrowed eyes. A black bear broke from underbrush on the opposite bank, ambled down to the river and drank. She was in no danger. Calico let loose a soft sigh. The bear couldn't see her, his sight was dreadful. But his sense of smell was keen. Downwind as he was, she judged he'd catch her scent in perhaps two minutes. But as if to give lie to her estimate, suddenly he reared up with a ferocious roar, sniffed the air, swinging his great shaggy head from side to side, then loped back into the underbrush.

"First one I've seen this year," came a voice behind her.

Calico leaped up and pivoted and found herself facing Judalon Tarrant. She swallowed a strangled gasp. His black eyes gleamed malevolently in his handsome face. Draped over his broad shoulders as though it were nothing more than a bath towel was the carcass of a hundred-pound deer. Her hand shot to the gun that lay between her breasts, snapping off the safety of the .22 without removing it from the leather.

Judalon grinned, unafraid. "Now, now, you ain't thinking of shootin' me, are you Calico Jones? Jobeth wouldn't take kindly to you putting me out of action."

"Leave Jobeth out of this," she said between clenched teeth. "You killed that deer out of season."

"A man's got to feed his family."

She wouldn't report him. He knew it. In Appalachia no one brought the law in to settle a dispute, no one tattled. Against outsiders mountain people closed ranks, not because a man hadn't done wrong, but because they brooked no interference in their lives.

"You've been sneaking about Talking Rock for more than deer. I know it was you who ransacked that house," she charged, flinging her arm to indicate the cabin behind him.

"You ain't never going to prove it."

"I'm not looking to." She eyed the rifle he held loosely in his huge hand. "Stop hunting on my land, and stop poking around—"

"You're mighty brave all of a sudden," he broke in slyly. "I seen the look on your face when I came up. What were you thinking on? That man you hauled out of the river? I noticed you didn't introduce me when I came to pick up my boys. Sweet on him, are you?"

She glared at him, noticing the subtle way he shifted the carcass on his shoulders, watched his eyes rake her menacingly, and noticed something else— the rise that was beginning to take shape below his belt pushing against his fitted denims. Her fingers gripped the gun butt. "Get off this mountain, Judalon," she hissed.

"You'd never use that thing on me," he said suavely.

"I will, and dump you where nobody'd ever find you." There was something in her tone, not a threat, but a fierce undulation—like hate.

"I'm leaving," he said, leering. "Got to get this deer skinned and jointed. But I've been meaning to warn you. Quit coming between me and Jobeth—you're puttin' ideas into her head."

Calico wished she'd refused the money she'd given

Jobeth to bond him out of jail—it was where he belonged. "I've never once brought your name up in conversation—you're not worth mentioning. I wouldn't waste my breath!"

"Kept me tucked away in your heart all these years?" His voice was suggestive, the bulge at his thighs growing.

"You make me sick!" She began to draw the gun from the holster.

"You'll have to shoot me in the back," he taunted, laughing as he turned and sauntered away from her.

"I hate you, Judalon Tarrant!" she screamed. But he didn't look back. She was trembling so violently her legs wouldn't hold her, and she fell to her knees, dry sobs choking her, closing up her throat. *One day . . . one day . . .* she promised herself.

She remained on her knees, prostrate for long minutes, remembering the wallet only as she rose to her feet. Her hunger for Irish took on an intense quality, an urgency—she needed something to blot out her shame, her guilt, renew the self-worth she'd discovered at his hands.

She tried to talk herself out of going to Atlanta. She could mail his purse. They had no common ground. There was too much city in him. She lived close to the land. Gold miners and scientists don't mix. If he was an engineer, a surveyor, or even another gold miner . . . but they had both been orphaned, hadn't they? They had that in common. And they had touched one another intimately.

In the end, the following morning she took Christian, protesting, down to Jeb and Winnie's.

On the drive to Atlanta she planned her approach. She would be polite, cool, not let him get the impression she was calling on him for any reason other than to return his wallet. She drove around Colony Square, where his apartment was located, a dozen times before she got up the courage to park under the shopping mall and walk over to his building. There was a uniformed doorkeeper standing behind a podiumlike desk. She asked for Irish McCaulley. The concierge shook his neatly trimmed head.

"Professor McCaulley's out of town." He had left a phone number and the name of the university at which he was staying if she'd like that information.

"No, no thank you." Irish was still leaving sign. That information was not meant for her, she knew. She would go back, leave his wallet with the doorkeeper, add a note asking after him. It was as close to begging his attention as her pride would allow.

"Calico! Calico Jones! I thought I recognized that head of red hair." She looked up, startled by the voice. "Phillip!" she exclaimed. "I—what are you...?"

He laughed. "I was just going to ask the same of you. I live here. Are you in Atlanta to shop? Visit?"

"A bit of shopping," she lied, stepping from the vehicle.

He took her elbow, propelling her along. "Well, this is wonderful. Come upstairs with me, let's have coffee at The Park, catch up on news. How's your grandfather? You had him in Emory? Ah, that's what you're doing here."

"No, he's home now and doing fine. I'm here to shop," she insisted, perpetuating the tale.

"You sure made an impression on Irish McCaulley, our resident scientist...." Her heart gave a small lurch. "Pulling him out of the river like that. Saved his life."

"He said that? You know him, but of course you do—"

"We're neighbors. Good friends, too, I like to think. I took him to pick up his car. We talked a bit."

"Oh." If he had mentioned her, just once, then he hadn't forgotten her. She felt a warm glow.

They went through the self-help line in the café and took their coffees to a table in the vast high-ceilinged lobby of the shopping mall. Phillip stirred sugar into his cup, staring at her. Calico had always fascinated him, yet when he'd gone to the mountains she had held herself aloof from his attentions. She had been friendly, offering sincere hospitality as only mountain people can. She'd even gone hunting with him on one occasion, but deep down he'd known a liaison with her would be unlikely. But it didn't stop him from dreaming for months after a hunting trip. He'd visualize her magnificent gray eyes, see them looking beyond the beyond, mysterious, and that swath of auburn hair. He'd never seen any to compare with it—unless you counted the photographs on the cover of women's magazines, and those never had the quality of naturalness that Calico projected. It wasn't that she seemed to loom larger than life itself; but that she was the very essence of life, of woman. There was something so different about her. Now he regretted that he'd never explored that difference. He sighed and smiled at her sheepishly.

"My mother taught me it wasn't good manners to stare, and I'm a married man," he observed ruefully.

She laughed. "You always were a big flirt, Phillip."

"Is that what you think of me?"

"I think you're a nice man."

"Gee—who wants to be nice?" He felt the urge to purge these half-guilty thoughts. It was as if he was being unfaithful to Ginny. "Say, are you staying in town overnight? I'd like you to meet my wife, our daughter, Sarah. We're having a few friends in tonight for drinks, a buffet supper—nothing fancy."

She hesitated. "No—I have to get back. Grampa's staying with—"

"You've got to come." Some odd feeling communicated itself to Phillip, as if Calico was in some manner desperate. He dismissed this thought. She had always been withdrawn, mysterious, those eyes hiding a deep well. And yet.... "Please," he urged quietly.

"Phillip. Thank you for asking, but truly, I—what would I have to talk about to your friends?"

"Good grief. Gold! You used to enthrall me with stories. Listen, remember that time we got rained out and you dragged me off to a sing and a clogging? This get-together is the same thing. Just regular people having a good time. They're wealthy, but not snobs, and I warrant none of them has ever held a gold nugget in his hands—they'll be fascinated."

She stiffened. "I don't want to be put on display like I'm some freak."

"You won't be," he assured her quickly. "Come early, meet Ginny and Sarah, and if you don't like anyone as they arrive, why you can leave." Calico registered his lazy appealing grin, but she had another thing on her mind.

Suppose I stay over, she thought, *Irish might return tonight or tomorrow. I'd get to see him, talk with him.* She gave Phillip a slow wonderful smile. "Are you still selling and buying real estate?"

"Yes, but what does that have to do with anything?"

"I was just noticing your powers of persuasion haven't flagged," she teased. "First you managed to talk grampa out of two acres and now here you are—"

"Then you'll come? Great. Six-thirty." He gave her a card with his apartment number and phone number.

Within the next thirty minutes Calico had registered at the Colony House Hotel at the opposite end of the mall and was browsing through Rich's department store, choosing a rust wool skirt, full cut, so that it swung entrancingly around her hips, and a beige blouse, daringly low cut. She also bought hose, a pair of heels that emphasized the turn of her ankle. An Estée Lauder makeup kit for redheads was added to her purchases and she begged a sample of Anais. She made a stop at the drugstore for hairbrush, tooth-brush, toothpaste and shampoo. In her eighth-floor room she napped, bathed, dressed, applied cosmetics, swirled her hair atop her head and wished she had bought a pair of earrings.

She looked in the mirror and liked what she saw. It came to her mind that no one in Lumpkin County had seen her in a dress since her senior-year prom— and that night, she recalled, had been a disaster. Her reflection looked like a stranger's, a person she didn't know.

She prowled the room, pensive, waiting for the pre-scribed six-thirty. She would not leave her room till then, and when she arrived at the apartments, she would only casually inquire if Irish McCaulley had yet returned. His mud-stained wallet was the only item she carried in her narrow leather purse.

10

"I'M CALICO JONES," she said to the short, attractive dark-haired woman dressed in a flowing maternity dress who opened the door to her.

Ginny Braeswood pulled Calico into the apartment with a breathless gaiety. "Oh, I'd know you any-where! Phillip has described you to me umpteen times. If he wasn't such a difficult man to tolerate, I'd be jealous, but I know no other woman could put up with him besides myself." She paused in the middle of the living room strewn with newspapers, toys clutter-ing every surface. "You wouldn't by any chance be an ordinary person who could lend a hand, would you? Time crept up on me and just when I thought every-thing was going right, Sarah got hungry. I had to stop to feed her, and then she needed a bath, and I've run out of ice, and the dips still need to be made and the silverware needs to be set out, the candles lit..." Ginny recited with a sigh. "I'm not exactly the most organized person I know."

"I'll be happy to help," Calico returned, warming to Ginny at once. "It'll keep me from feeling—"

"Wonderful! You can be co-hostess. Come meet Sarah first. Phillip's rocking her to sleep—then...." She heaved another heavy sigh, glancing around the room, visualizing an order that it hadn't known since Sarah's birth.

Calico pronounced Sarah a darling, and then set about in her efficient way to bring order to the chaos in the living room. Ginny greeted guests, dragging each couple to the kitchen where Calico was now filling platters with food. The wives stayed to help Calico, while Phillip carried the men off for drinks.

One woman laughed as Ginny disappeared. "It's always like this when we get an invitation to Ginny's. You never know whether to wear your best dress or an apron! She can get more work out of the president of a company than the board of directors."

"Yes," agreed a woman named Judy, adding with a grin, "and if you happen to be that president and don't make the trek into Sarah's room first, Phillip'll buy up your company the following day and fire your arse!"

Music was put on the stereo, voices mingled. Calico could not remember all the names, but she found herself laughing at jokes, visiting with the wives, talking recipes, explaining how she cooked on a wood stove. The women were awed.

"It must be wonderful not to have utility bills," exclaimed Judy.

"I would dearly love a utility bill," Calico said with a laugh. "Especially when it comes time to chop and stack wood."

When they discovered that she was a gold miner, they couldn't get enough, drowning her with questions. Phillip had been right. Conversation never flagged, his guests were interested and interesting.

In one way Calico was part of those around her, part of the gaiety, the laughter, yet in her mind she was as separated as though she were on another planet, another level, invisible. When she'd arrived at the apartment building the doorkeeper, a different one this time, gave her the same information as the first. Professor McCaulley had not returned from Kansas City. The party had been in full swing now for more than an hour, and her enthusiasm had waned.

It was still early, only a few minutes after eight, yet she contemplated making her adieus and leaving, returning to Lumpkin County. There were more people filing into the apartment. She glanced up and froze. Irish McCaulley was poised on the threshold. It was a moment, an eternity, before he took in the room. His eyes passed over her. He shook his head as if to dislodge a vision, and looked again.

For a moment they stared at one another, wordless. Calico looked stunning in a natural way, unaided by fancy dressmakers. There was an allure to her face, the cast so enigmatic, her silvery eyes glowing as if all the secrets in the universe lay hidden behind them. There was a quality to her, a golden depth, as if she brought with her the spirit of Talking Rock Mountain—freshness and wonder—and Irish nearly knocked people over making his way across the room to her.

"I thought I was seeing things," he said, leaning close to inhale the scent of her, a subtle language that sped picture words across his mind, and he touched her on her arm, proving that she was indeed before him, flesh and blood. "You're the last person in the world I expected to find here."

"Phillip and I are old friends...."

They devoured one another with their eyes while the seconds ticked by silently. His gaze dropped to the softly curved ivory breasts. "Stupid of me not to make the connection," he murmured. "How's your grandfather?"

"Better. He's at home now."

He wanted to maintain an aura of control near her, but he felt so undone, unraveled, incomplete. The part of him that seemed to stay perpetually aflame began to rise. It took him an agonizing moment to dispel the activity in his inguinal area. "What brings you to Atlanta?"

You. "I had to do some shopping. I found your wallet—"

"So it was you who asked about me downstairs! I
couldn't figure out...."

"Yes, and then I ran into Phillip and here I am."

He wanted to take her into his arms desperately, get
rid of this ache in his loins. He hadn't had a moment's
peace since he'd met her. "I'm here to meet some
people," he said, feeling like a fool. Then he gave up
all pretense. "Let's get a drink." He put his arm
around her waist. "I've tried to get you out of my
mind."

She looked startled, scanning his face anxiously.
"Why?"

"You scare me. You're so full of subtleties. My scientific mind likes everything in sequence, logical. I
wanted to drop you a note, tell you thank-you—I
didn't even know your address. I know nothing about
you."

"You know everything about me," she said softly,
for his ears alone as they reached the wet bar. He
made them drinks.

"How old are you, anyway?"

"Thirty. But what difference—" Phillip was at his
elbow.

"Irish, you snuck in here behind my back," he observed in a tone that was at once accusing and
amused. "How was your trip? Kansas City? Get a job
offer?"

"They gave me something to think about."

"So did I," Phillip mused. "Have you opened your
mail yet?"

Irish looked puzzled. "No. I dumped my bags and
came straight upstairs. Why?"

"I think you ought to check you mail," Phillip said
mysteriously.

"You know something I don't?"

"I do. Via my family grapevine. But it's not something for me to announce—I mean—hell, I don't know what I mean, just go downstairs and check your mail."

Irish turned to Calico. "Come with me?"

She nodded quietly. "Will we be long?"

There was no one in the room for them. The music, the laughter, the tinkling of glass, murmuring voices were all outside the realm of their world. Phillip watched this transformation with growing puzzlement. But, he too, was being ignored.

"I think we will be," Irish said. And the naked emotion in his green eyes was no longer veiled by thick dark lashes.

It took perhaps two minutes for them to make their way along the carpeted corridor, call up the elevator, enter and emerge, returning to the twin of the Braeswood apartment only one floor below. As if by tacit agreement they neither spoke nor touched on the journey. Fiery need and hunger rendered the air thick between them, primitive urges canted from a far memory in the brain. A monumental force no mere mortal could withstand.

Calico observed him, studied him, drinking in his hawklike features as he unlocked the door and stepped in, waiting for her to follow. He flicked a wall switch as she moved up the foyer steps. An incandescent glow illuminated a silk lamp shade decorated with Oriental fans. He locked the door. It was safe to talk, to touch, to breathe.

"You've had the stitches out of your head," she said.

"Yes." He wasn't interested in such inane talk. His suitcase stood just at the top of the foyer, his mail where he'd tossed it on the red-lacquered table. He ignored it. "I have you to myself," he said in a husky timbre.

"I—where's Sam?"

"Upstairs. Ginny's watching him for me."

"I didn't see him." Her lips parted, there seemed to be a sad lack of oxygen in the air.

"She probably had him hidden away in one of the back rooms. They bought the place next to theirs—I don't want to talk about Sam or the Braeswoods just now." He drew a trembling finger down the curve of her cheek. "I've never seen you in a dress." He was only murmuring now, his voice low, caressing. His hands slipped to her hair, removing pins, letting it cascade down her back like a river of flowing copper. He buried his fingers in the silken mass, drawing it over her breasts and began to unbutton her blouse. A strand caught on a button; he tried to untangle it.

Calico laughed. "Idiot. You're making it worse. We'll have to make love with our clothes on."

"No."

"Get the scissors then."

"I hate for you to cut a single strand—"

"Why? Are you afraid it'll bring on a curse?"

"I'm under your spell now. Why else do I feel so driven?" The lock of hair was snipped, the scissors set aside, her arms slipped beneath his suit jacket, sliding up his shirt, her fingertips meeting no encumbrances. She pulled back. "You've had the tape off your ribs, too. So soon."

"It was driving me crazy, like you're driving me crazy. Did anyone ever tell you that you talk too much?" he whispered as he bent his mouth to hers. His tongue was hot and moist, bespeaking his inarticulate longing, thrusting into her with a savagery that took away what little breath remained in her lungs. His hands were like nomads, ungovernable in their wanton plundering of her body, and after some moments he realized they were still clothed and he led her into his bedroom and undressed her slowly, prolonging the agonizing urgency that made her flesh burn, her breasts swell, her nipples ache for his ravaging tongue. He disrobed, throwing his clothes over the wooden valet, and all the change in his pockets fell to the carpet. He was swollen with need and Calico took him into her.

THE BEDROOM WAS ALL DIMNESS and shadows, a white slice of moon slanting across Irish's huge bed, where a languor prevailed. He reached a hand lazily to the bedside lamp, switching it on. His expression was one of thoughtful introspection. He loved Calico Jones. It did not come upon him with any sudden sense of clarity. He just acknowledged that it was there inside him, as if it belonged there. He glanced at her. She had been watching him in the moonlight. With a curious enigmatic smile she looked away again. Did she know what he was thinking? Was she thinking it herself?

"Shouldn't you check your mail and shouldn't we go back upstairs?" she asked in a softly satisfied voice.

"In a few minutes."

She turned toward him. "Will they know—what we've been doing?"

He laughed. "No doubt, but they'll have the good manners not to mention it." He put his arms around her and held her close. "I can't get over how you looked tonight, no different and yet—different. You seem to fit with all those people up there."

"And do I fit with you?" There was a quaver in her voice that held promise.

"I think you know the answer to that," he murmured, and smiled. "All I'm saying is—"

"You think where I live, where I was born is primitive and that this is civilization—you're surprised that I took to your civilized world, is that it?"

"Partly," he acknowledged. "Are you reading my mind?"

She ran her fingers through the hair on his chest. His skin was raw, but healing where he had removed the tape. "No, but I'm curious why you're asking."

"Would you ever leave your world, your mountain?"

Her hand fell back to the bed. She thought it was inevitable that they come together, stay together, but she'd never considered that it would be away from Talking Rock. "No. I've thought about it. Packed my bags often enough and got down to the foot, then turned around and went back. I can't explain it to you, my life is there; I count on the mountain."

"For what?"

She turned and lay on her back, staring at the ceiling, her hands composed and folded over her abdomen. "Everything."

Irish felt himself to be rootless. Was he being fair, asking her to leave her own roots behind—he couldn't finish the thought. He still didn't belong. The spectre of Sister Antonio loomed in his mind. But what was there for him on Talking Rock? "How do you manage, day in and day out without necessities?"

Her laughter was low and throaty, teasing. "Necessities are air, water, food, shelter—all else is luxury."

"Electricity and running water are luxuries?" There was a light trace of sarcasm in his tone.

"I'd love to have electricity, but Grampa's against it. About a dozen years ago I got him to agree to it in one of his weak—no, drunken—moments," she said truthfully, "and he's not a man to go back on his word, so the power company began a survey on where to set out the poles. Grampa told the crew to stick to the road that winds around the mountain, but they refused, said they were going to lay the wire the shortest distance, and drove their truck right over an old mine shaft. It collapsed. The survey crew got out okay, but the shaft was filled with quicksand and the truck was lost. The power company sent grampa a bill for it saying he should've warned them of hazards. He sent them a dime with a note for them to call him about it."

"But you don't have a phone."

"I know. That's how grampa's mind works—when it works." she muttered under her breath sadly. "Anyway, grampa and the utility company have been feuding ever since."

"What did you mean, *when* your grampa's mind works? I though you said he was fine."

"He fades in and out of reality, not so much as he did. Jerry says grampa's shell-shocked, or scared, that seeing you triggered it."

Irish shot up. "Me? I've never seen the old man before in my life!" He paused, then added suspiciously, "Who's this Jerry, anyway?"

"Dr. Bass, from Emory. He made me go through everything and when I did he seemed to think you—"

"Being a physican myself, I know the mind works in mysterious ways, but that kind of diagnosis is a joke," he snapped.

"I'm not blaming you," Calico said swiftly.

"I didn't say you were." He swung his legs over the side of the bed, dragging the sheets with him. She grabbed at a corner, covering her nakedness. His mood swing troubled her. She didn't like it.

"You told me you were a scientist, now you're saying—"

"I finished medical school, but I never took a residency, I went straight into teaching and research." He was putting on a robe he had taken from the closet. Calico wrapped the sheet about her more securely, trying to undo his mood with a shrug and a smile.

"But you just want to do the research part?" she said, aiming for a less controversial subject than Christian.

"Yes." His answer was sharp.

"So you can be your own boss."

He was taking slacks off a hanger, a turtleneck shirt from a drawer. "Exactly."

"I like being my own boss, too, that's one more thing we have in common."

He looked at her then. "Are you counting?"

"Sort of." She hesitated. "You look for all the ways we're different. I look for all the ways we're alike."

"Is that important?"

Calico was frozen with apprehension. For the first time it occurred to her that there was something hidden, something lurking deep within him that he would not share with her. An emotion, almost of pain, went through her. "Isn't it?"

He gave her a brooding look and went into the bathroom.

Thirty minutes later, Calico, too, was bathed and dressed, standing before a steamy mirror repinning her hair when Irish, in the front room, let go with a happy whoop. "What was that all about?" she asked, smiling at his exuberance, joining him as she set the last pin into place.

He waved a letter in a decisive arc. "I've won an award for some work I did last year, and a nice bit of change comes with it."

"That's wonderful. Are you so well-known, then?"

He laughed, a self-deprecating sort of laugh to camouflage the pride he was feeling. "Not me so much as my work, but this couldn't have come at a better time." The doorbell chimed an interruption that caused a glimmer of rancor to cross his face. "That's probably Phillip," he said, moving toward the entrance with an indolent stride. "He's probably wondering where we've been. Damn! He should've telephoned."

But the moment Irish swung open the door, Calico knew it wasn't Phillip. She elevated her gaze beyond Irish's shoulder to get a glimpse, and an icy hand seemed to grip her whole body. A woman's voice floated up from the foyer well.

"Irish, you nasty man, you've had the locks changed on our apartment."

He stood there, a look of pained incredulity on his face, feeling as if he'd just been gored by a bull. He lost all sense of where he was, whom he was with; confusion flared in his eyes. Then it was obliterated by a deep encompassing anger. "This is *my* apartment, Belle. What are doing here?"

"The errant wife returns," she said, laughing nasally, lifting her lips to his.

Wife! The word exploded in Calico's brain. She thought she was going to be sick. But Irish was hers, and hers alone! Could the fates have been so wrong?

"Returns! Hell!" Irish was saying with violent emphasis. "We're divorced!" Belle ignored him, simply brushed past him and moved swiftly up the stairs. Seeing Calico, she stopped dead in her tracks.

Calico stared at Belle as if her eyes would burst; a woman her own age, elegantly dressed, milk-white skin, tinted hair beautifully styled, and she felt the hostility spewing in her direction before Belle turned back to Irish.

"Oh, I'm so sorry to interrupt a tête-à-tête," she drawled in a voice that set the lie to her apology. "But, Irish darling, we're not divorced."

He reeled, thunderstruck. "What kind of a game are you playing this time, Belle? It won't work. You're not welcome here. I signed the divorce papers." He ground out the words, pacing them, flashing a look at Calico as he spoke and his insides turned to lead.

"Oh, you did do that darling," she agreed airily.
"but I didn't file them after all. Daddy is having a bit
of a problem at the bank and he thought a divorce
would fuel the scandal."

"Scandal! Your father thrives on it," Irish sneered,
wondering if what Belle said could be true, knowing
that it had to be or she wouldn't be here, back in his
life unless it was.

"Not this time, Irish," she said firmly, then gave
her attention over to Calico again, saying acidly,
"Sorry, my dear, but my husband is not quite available. You were just leaving?"

Calico bristled. She was riddled with despair, yet she
had been too long her own woman to run from this
gussied-up creature who stood before her. She looked
to Irish. "Is this true? Are you a married man?"

"No!" Then, "Maybe, but just on paper." He crossed
to her put his arm around her. "I'll work this out—"

"No, you won't," Belle injected, snarling. "We're
married and we will be as long as I have any say, so
get your little tramp out of my house."

Irish whirled on her. "Shut up, Belle!" he flung at
her viciously. Never in his life had he felt so violently
angry, yet so utterly helpless.

Calico reached for her purse, took out his wallet
and tossed it onto the red table. "I shouldn't have
come here," she declared, looking directly into his
green, green eyes. "Your wife and I have one thing in
common, Irish—we don't like to share. Give my re-
gards to Phillip and Ginny, will you?" She moved toward the door, back straight, passing Belle without a
glance.

"Calico! Wait!" He followded her into the corridor.
"I need you. You fill me with—God! I can't name it,
but I want to keep on seeing you. Belle means noth—"

"You ask too much of me," she told him, avoiding
his eyes. "I'm going home."

THE ELEVATOR CLOSED upon her and Irish just stood there, feeling as though his life had drained out of him. The vacuum it left began to fill with unutterable anger, an anger so wild, so ungovernable, so deep that it altered his face almost completely. When he reentered his apartment, Belle's eyes filled with real fear.

"You had better tell me what this is all about," he said, his voice guttural. "And so help me! One lie, one tiny lie...." He left the words hanging as he stalked the apartment, circling her. Belle tracked him carefully with her eyes.

"It's true what I said," she whispered. "Daddy said I couldn't sign the papers and have our attorney file them. He controls my money, he threatened me. He said if I divorced you I'd never get another cent—"

Irish exploded. "Why, dammit? Amos has never liked me from the moment he set eyes on me. I can still remember the way he recoiled—those narrow beady suspicious banker's eyes looking at me like I was the embodiment of evil, like I was going to ask him for a loan. Always sneeering at my past, saying an orphan wasn't good enough for his little Belle. If you think I'm going to believe he doesn't want me out of your family...." Irish crossed the room to Belle, taking her by her shoulders, shaking her until real tears began to moisten her cheeks. When he saw them he stopped, pushing her away from him, then looking at his hands with revulsion as though he had just dipped them into filth.

He breathed deeply, sucking air into his lungs, an attempt to calm the savage rage, the violent frustration saturating his pores. He knew what he wanted. But there was in him an honesty, a conscience, and he had to ask "Do you want to make another go, do you want to try on our marriage again?" He hated the quaver in his voice.

Belle's head jerked around. Looking at him, her

eyes filled with pure contempt. "No. I hate you. I hate being here. I want excitement, travel...." Her lips curled. "There's already another man."

He felt like he was rising up from ashes. "So why are you here, Belle? What instructions do you have from dear old Amos? He knows everything about me. He had me investigated after we were married. He thought I wouldn't find out but a friend of mine in hospital worked in personnel.... What was your conversation with Amos exactly?"

Belle shrugged her elegant shoulders. "We just talked. He told me that a divorce wouldn't be a good idea right now. If I considered it he'd throw me out, cut off my trust. He controls the family's money. I couldn't live without money, Irish. You know that..." She was pleading, whining in that harsh nasal way of hers.

He turned away in disgust.

"I promise you, we mostly talked! Daddy wondered if you'd ever found your father; he wondered if you were making progress in your work down here."

"Progress!" Irish laughed, a bitter sound. "Tell him yes, tell him I got fired. And you get back to Boston and you tell him I want this divorce."

Belle crumbled. "I—I can't."

For days Calico was alternately angry and morose. She grew edgy and irritable, and Christian, when he was alert and knew better, kept out of her way. Jobeth came up to the mountain once, leaving after only a few minutes. "You're not fit company for the devil," she stated, stalking off to her truck in a huff.

Calico felt betrayed and was powerless to do anything about it. She cursed herself, cursed Irish and cursed fate that had thrown him into her life. But most especially, she cursed Belle McCaulley.

The weather was dismal, threatening—one of those times when the sun refused to give solace while gray clouds perversely held their moisture. The wind blew down the sluice, gusting one minute, caressing the next, as if nature were taking her cue from Calico.

Swamped with restlessness, Calico tried to rid herself of an electric energy by working. She panned for gold on the riverbank. Rock and pit gravel cut into her knees, but she was inured to the discomfort— it hardly registered on her senses. Without Irish everything in her life seemed so trivial and unsatisfactory.

And that wasn't the only thing that plagued her. She saw phallic symbols in every tree, in the shape of clouds, in the excrescence of rock—all reminding her forcefully of Irish McCaulley; erotic bits that she deemed wanton and for which there was no relief but the man himself. She was almost, but not quite enjoying her misery. How he was going to get out of his marriage, she couldn't imagine, but he must. He just must. For if he didn't, there could be nothing between them—ever.

She took her frustration out on the mud in her pan, kneading it savagely, squeezing it, crushing it with her strong fingers, watching it being swept away by the river current, and it took the hated amorphous shape of Belle.

Filling the pan, propping it an inch or so under water, plucking out larger stones, swirling black sands, tweezing up the gold flecks was familiar ritual requiring no thought. Her mind was at Colony House, at his apartment. She didn't see the clouds lowering, the mists descending upon gray green Appalachian peaks, she didn't see the old hen bring her yellow fluffed chicks down to drink only yards from where she panned, and she didn't hear the footfalls as a man approached.

"Making mud pies?" he drawled amusingly. Calico grabbed up the gold pan, ready to dispense justice, pivoting so that jagged pebbles ground painfully into her knees.

"Dr. Bass!" He was dressed warmly, wearing hiking boots, old blue jeans, a knapsack and bedroll packed upon his wide shoulders. His eyes were red rimmed as if from lack of sleep though his face was freshly shaven.

"You do recall inviting me?" he asked, a trifle hesitant. "You didn't mention a specific date, but...." He lapsed into sheepish apology.

"You're a fool to come here," she said, recovering from the start he gave her. "But I won't run you off." She bent to gather her equipment, brushing mud from her knees, knowing he was watching her intently. "How'd you find us?"

"Caught a ride with a hog farmer below Gainsville. He brought me right to the foot of the mountain.

When I mentioned your name, he...you seem to be pretty famous."

Calico winced. "What's famous is the way my neighbors loosen their tongues. Did you hitchhike all the way from Atlanta?"

"I did. I just came off a seventy-two-hour shift, so I'm not in the best of shape. I have four days off. Can you put up with me until Sunday?"

"If we can't, I'll point you down the mountain."

"Fair enough." He didn't try to hide the relief in his voice. Calico liked him for that. "How's your grandfather these days?"

"Right this minute he's napping." She balanced the shovel and pick over her shoulder and set off up the incline, Jerry Bass in step with her. "He has his lucid moments, but I never know what he's going to do when he does. He's cut the cast off his ankle, and he and our cousin Jeb, who's as old and stubborn as grampa, have been whittling toes, dozens of them—trying to get some to fit. He's drinking more than usual. Other times he just sits and stares into the fire." She sighed wearily. "Why? Do you still think you can cure him?"

Jerry was reflective, choosing his words carefully. "The mind is a funny thing. It latches onto a painful or harrowing experience and builds it up into something so grotesque we won't even consider its existence." He was silent a moment, then continued softly. "When that happens, it's my job to break it down piece by piece, make it acceptable, easier to face. I think that's what fascinates me, the way each of us sees ourself. What you or I might consider shameful about ourselves, others see as virtue. Self-esteem is a wondrous thing when we have it." His thoughts seemed to turn inward. "Loss of it is as debilitating as a cancer."

Calico stopped in midstride. "You think my grampa

has lost his self-esteem?" There was disbelief in her voice.

Jerry shrugged. "I don't know. He killed a man, didn't he?"

"Yes, but he said the man deserved to die."

"You told me that before. Do you know exactly what happened?"

Calico shook her head and her gray eyes glinted hard as stone. "It had to do with my grandmother's death and I've never asked. When I was little I was curious, but as I got older ... well there can be so many things between a man and a woman ...." Her voice trailed off as they resumed their trek and reached the cabin.

"Do you think you could get him to talk about it."

"Is it important?" She would love to have her grandfather whole—have him be once again the garrulous old man who nagged her to marry, fussed at her to hurry at chores and drank a pint of homemade brandy for breakfast. Jerry nodded sagely. "Then I'll ask him," she said.

"Let him get used to me first." He touched her arm as she dumped pick and shovel and pan on the porch. "Just say I'm a friend you met at the hospital."

"Is that fair?" she asked, taken aback.

"People give up their secrets freely to strangers— I'll explain it to you sometime."

Calico prayed silently, *Please, Jerry Bass, please know what you are doing.*

The grayness on the mountain had seeped inside the cabin. It was dim and shadowy, so Calico hurried to light a lamp. When its soft golden light lifted to the beamed ceiling, Jerry Bass shrugged the knapsack from his shoulders as he pivoted slowly, taking it all in. The wall of books, the great stone fireplace, the huge dining table, the wood-burning stove, the wall of shelves that held row after row of food, store-bought and home-canned vegetables, jellies, soups and meats. "This takes me back to my grandmother's," he said quietly, with a kind of reverence. "The woodsmoke and kerosene evoke memories I thought I'd forgotten. Did you do all that canning?" he asked with a gravity of a man who recognized the amount of work it represented.

"I helped some, but my cousin's wife, Winnie, did most of it," replied Calico. "She keeps a garden that would feed an army and shares it with us."

He sprang to the shelves, inspecting the rows more closely. His fingers trailed over the jars like those of a blind person reading Braille. "Look at the dates on these," he murmured awestruck. "Eighteen eighty-three, and this one—1798. They're worth a fortune. I collect glass; it's a hobby."

"We never throw anything away. Canning jars are more useful to us filled than empty, decorating a cabinet."

Jerry laughed and some of the tiredness left his eyes. "Hey, I'm an old country boy. I can stoke a fire, cook too. Suppose I help you with supper?" He began taking jars off the shelves, selecting the most antique, setting them on the stove.

Calico was loathe to stop him, but her practical nature intervened. "You can cook if you want to, but don't think about emptying all those—there's only the three of us. Most of it would just have to be tossed out to the chickens."

He gave her a boyish grin. "Waste not, want not."

"There's a box in the shed out back with a bunch of jars. Their rims are cracked. You can go through them and take as many as you can carry."

"Wonderful. They'll be my fee."

"I didn't hire you," Calico said enigmatically. "You volunteered."

He bowed slightly, a thin trace of humor in the

mocking gesture. "Bless my grandmother; I'd forgotten how blunt, how quick to the point a mountain woman can be."

"One of my failings," she said with a smile. "And I hope you don't attach any significance to that." But she was reminded of Irish, his similar comment, and the smile vanished beneath a troubled expression.

"Who're you talking to, Calico?" Christian called from his bed.

"Excuse me?" she said to Jerry Bass. "I'd better let grampa know we have company."

When Christian shuffled into the living room a short time later, Jerry approached him and said without preamble, "I met you and Calico at Emory. I both intrigued me. If I get on your nerves, just let me know and I'll leave."

Calico was abashed that Jerry was direct himself. She had been tiptoeing around her grandfather for fear she would say or do something that would distress him. Yet, she would come to learn that during the time Jerry was on Talking Rock not once did Christian descend into that dark gloom that took him out of her reach. The young doctor made Christian laugh, telling little jokes on himself, and for that she was grateful. There hadn't been any laughter on Talking Rock for a long, long time. And some of the restlessness went out of her.

Christian studied Jerry's countenance. It seemed to emit a kind of nonjudgmental acceptance that forged a personal link. Jerry's gestures, his stance, his smile seemed to be saying, *I know your secrets and I like you anyway, so come on, throw in your lot with the human race.* Christian shifted his weight on the crutches. "Calico tells me your were raised country. Any skill with a whittling knife?"

"I've carved out my share of flutes and whistles, repaired the plunger on a butter churn or two...."

The old man nodded his shaggy head vigorously. "Mayhap I won't run you off too soon," he said in his thick gravelly voice. "Come on outside to the wood-pile with me."

IT SEEMED TO CALICO that Jerry had no more than ar-rived when it was almost time for him to go. He had ingratiated his way into their lives well and was ex-tremely comfortable to be around. She wished that he had been born a woman because she felt he alone was capable of understanding all the turmoil that raged in her, but he was a man, and she dared not mention a single word of Judalon, or even Irish.

"I never did get around to helping you do any cooking," he said on Saturday night. He was helping her with the supper dishes. He washed, she dried, be-cause she knew where everything went. Christian had set the fire in the hearth and now lounged con-tent on the sofa packing his pipe.

"I know. Next time, maybe."

"Next time. Is that an invitation?" he asked. "You wouldn't mind having me return?"

"Thanksgiving is coming up in a couple of weeks..." she said by way of answering.

He frowned. "Residents don't get holidays, but hold it open."

"Anytime then."

He shook suds from his hands and leaned on the great ironstone sink, glancing out the window, taking in the panorama of the mountain. The sun was cast-ing a last fiery finger of red over the landscape, and even as Calico followed his gaze darkness began to close in. "This view would cost you a hundred thou-sand dollars if it was in Aspen or the hills around Los Angeles," he said.

"You've traveled there?" Calico asked, lifting a dish from the scarred wooden drainboard. Jerry had revealed little of his past to her; she hadn't asked.

"Yes, but I'm not talking so much about where I've been, there just seems to be something about your place that makes me feel closer to God. I guess you can't put any price tag on that."

The plate in Calico's hand slipped, shattering on the floor. Jerry looked at her sharply. "Did I say something to upset you?" He stooped to help her pick up the shards, inhaling the scent of her, noticing the mysterious cachet to her face that had now closed him out. He hadn't been lying when he had admitted to himself that he'd been drawn to North Georgia as much by the granddaughter as the grandfather.

"No, it just slipped," she replied.

His intuition was working, stabbing and he asked, "You don't believe in God?"

"That's personal." She spoke the words harshly, turning away from him to put the broken platter into a bucket.

"It's my business to ask personal questions," he reminded her quietly.

Her entire body went rigid. "Not of me."

"No...not of you." He paused, looking into the depths of her silvery eyes, then got himself in hand. "What's the usual after dinner on a Saturday night? Do we have coffee, tea, something stronger?"

"I'll have tea, you and grampa can have brandy," she said, and the awkward moment sank into oblivion.

FLICKERING DANCING IMAGES cast by lamp and firelight on the whitewashed walls melted like phantoms above their heads into the dark and soaring space of the beamed ceiling. Conversation had lagged, becoming desultory, yet there was something utterly palpable in the air. Calico sensed it as she sat on a wooden stool near the hearth brushing her hair from its confining braids. Jerry sat in an overstuffed chair sipping brandy, his eyelids drooping. Her grandfather was drawing on his pipe, blowing out clouds of smoke, the rich pungency of tobacco mingling with pine and burning resin. Calico could not fathom which of the men was projecting this tension. She just knew it lay there among them.

Unobserved, Jerry watched Calico through slitted eyes. Her auburn hair seemed to come alive as it reflected coppery flames shooting up the chimney. His hooded gaze strayed to Christian. The old man, too, was watching Calico.

Wire taut, Jerry continued his scrutiny, wanting desperately to find the key that would open the abyss in the old man. He would never forget the first time he had seen Christian Jones. Iron-gray hair long about his ears, beard, full and unkempt, that met the same grayness in his mustache, and thick eyebrows beneath a bulging forehead. Lying helpless in the hospital bed, his ankle in a cast, his toes crudely amputated, wandering in and out of a near-catatonic state. Yet beneath that helplessness had risen a spirit of determination, and Jerry felt privileged to have seen a glimpse, if ephemeral, of the fragile inner man—a quaking urgency that let itself be known. The same urgency was evident in Calico, but then, his attraction for her.... He forced his mind back to Christian. Eighty-two years old, unafraid of death, and still driven to—to what?

The old man shifted, rearranging his injured foot propped on a small three-legged stool. His gaze was riveted on Calico. "My Lucy had hair like that." He spoke softly in his deep voice as if he were mesmerized.

Jerry came alert, holding his breath.

Calico answered from some faraway world of her own. "I know, grampa, you've told me hundreds of times." She dropped the brush into her lap, lacing her fingers together, leaning toward Christian so that her profile was set aflame by burning embers. "Doc Willis told me something I didn't know. He said the day grandmother Lucy died, you were off delivering him. He's always wished since, that he'd been born another day."

"Time doesn't erase memories like it ought to," Christian answered, handing his pipe to her. She knocked it against a stone in the fireplace. Christian watched the dead ashes drift into the fire, taking back the pipe absently, mechanically unscrewing the stem and blowing through it to clear away trapped saliva. "Did I never tell you about that day?" He began the process of packing his pipe again.

"No, I don't think you have, or I would've remembered." She darted a glance at Jerry to see if he was awake and listening. His head was thrown back on the chair, his eyes closed, but his lids fluttered and he dropped an elusive smile.

Christian stared into the soot-streaked hearth and before his eyes the dying flames took shape, old shapes, old pains. He thought he was looking back into hell; no one else in the room mattered. Jerry Bass did not exist. Calico did not exist. For how could they? It was before they were born.

"Lucy...." He savored her name, letting it roll over his tongue. "Lucy was a good woman, a good mother, a churchgoer. Lordy did she like church. She belonged to a tiny religious sect of snake handlers." He paused remembering, and a cold shudder worked its way up his spine. "Poisonous snakes, mostly copperheads, moccasins and rattlers...."

Calico's stomach lurched. She had a feeling of repugnance laced with fear. "Grampa," she said, but he seemed not to hear. She shot a look, a nonverbal plea to Jerry Bass: *Will this hurt him? Is it all right for him to talk about this?* His nod was almost imperceptible.

Her grandfather had returned to his past, a half century ago and he pulled Calico and Jerry with him. "I'd seen four- and five-year-olds get worked up into a psychotic hypnosis, brought on by all that shouting and singing and speaking in tongues, and grab up a snake. It didn't bear thinking about. The preacher's name was Vernon.... He was the nicest man outside the pulpit...give you the last quarter out of his pocket, but my God! He could stir those people with his preaching.

"Lucy always handled the snakes when they were brought into the service." Suddenly Christian's voice took on power, becoming deep and resonant. Calico started, Jerry felt the adrenaline begin to pour into his veins.

"They shall take up serpents; and if they drink any deadly thing it shall not hurt them; they shall lay hands on the sick and they shall recover." His voice dropped to a whisper. "My Lucy didn't recover."

"If you got bit and died, you were damned. The last thing Lucy heard before going into a coma was Vernon telling her she was a sinner, telling her she was damned, telling her she was descending into hell to be consumed by the devil.... That's what I couldn't forgive him for.... Standing over like that, raving—" His voice cracked and between his thick fingers, the pipe stem snapped in two.

Calico opened her mouth to speak; Jerry silenced her with a wave of his hand. The seconds ticked by while the wind whistled eerily around the corners of the cabin, and there was the muted rumble of falling rock. The memory was too much for Christian. He pulled himself up on his uninjured foot, reaching for his crutches, then shambled slowly across the room, past the oaken table to the cookstove. He took down the jar of peach brandy and consumed several ounces. Fortified by alcohol, he moved back to the sofa, taking up the story as if nothing had happened.

"We buried her the next day. I was blind with grief and hate. No one could calm me. Winnie and Jeb took McKenzie." He bent his head toward Calico, not actually looking at her. "McKenzie was your father."

"Yes, I know," she murmured.

"I thought about killing myself and then I thought about killing Vernon. I don't recall the following week; I don't remember going over to the church that Sunday morning, or waiting for Vernon in the shack out back where the snakes were kept in boxes and sacks. But they found me leaning against the door. Vernon was inside with all the snakes writhing and loose. He was dead or dying.... The judge gave me twenty years—said it was a crime of passion. I served every one, and never regretted them—it's not likely that I ever will...."

Calico swung her glance from her grandfather to Jerry. He had a look of keen anticipation on his face that surprised her. Hadn't Christian told them everything?

"There was... was another death..." Christian began, then stopped to rub a gnarled and veined hand over the heavy bones about his temple and eyes. At once Jerry leaned forward, quickened interest on his face, but Calico could stand no more.

"Come on, grampa," she said, "I'll help you to bed."

His eyes fastened on her as he shook himself from lethargy. "No." The word was sheathed in pride. He hauled himself to his feet, adjusted the crutches, their rubber tips giving off a thumping cadence as he shuffled toward his room. The second his door was solidly closed Jerry spun on Calico.

"Why did you stop him?" he asked, tight lipped. "He was getting close to something."

"Grampa was tired. That other death; it had to be my father's. I know it troubles him. He only met my mother once, while he was still in prison and that was before I was born."

"We don't *know* that." He slapped a fist into his palm, extolling frustration. "Damn!"

"I won't let you push grampa too far," she said firmly. "He'll go into one of his black moods and I never know if he's going to come out of them. Besides, I couldn't listen to more. I—I have such a feeling of things lost, never to be retrieved."

"Yes," he answered wearily. "Our past deeds, the life behind us already lived...we can't reclaim them. That your grandfather is alive at all today is proof of his superb endurance. Have faith."

"In you?" It was a sarcastic barb.

"In him, or whatever it is that you believe in. Don't you see," Jerry said urgently, "he wants to end it; he wants to talk about it."

She chafed at his words. "End what?"

"His pain, his inner suffering—this second death is the key, I'm sure of it."

"You make it sound so easy. I'm telling you, there's never been another death, not one that he had anything to do with."

"He was fifty-two years old before you came into his life, and he's lived most of the past thirty years as a recluse, with you. A lot can happen to a man in his first half century."

"You're fishing." She poked at the fire, stirring the smoldering embers, watching sparks fly up the flue.

"Am I? Have you ever done something that you wished you hadn't or had anything ever happened to you that you didn't want to happen? I can see by the look on your face the answer is yes," he said, quietly triumphant. "It's the same with Christian. When something hurts, what do you do? Go back and review the event itself? Or the moment before? *Before*, always *before*. You see, up until the instant of a happening we see ourselves in control—during the happening or whatever we lose control, blot it out of our minds...but after...that's what starts us playing the 'what if' game in our minds."

"So?" She refused to give an inch.

"So we begin to ask ourselves what's the meaning of life? Our strong points suddenly become our weaknesses."

"You're not making any sense to me."

He smiled with a truculent assurance. "No?"

"No. I'll get you another quilt. It's colder tonight."

Despite dedication to his work there was in Jerry Bass a bit of whimsy and Calico was like a magnet. He followed her into her room, standing at the bottom of the ladder that led to the loft while she rummaged in a trunk. "Your bed looks plenty enough for two," he said suggestively.

Calico slammed the lid of the trunk, the expression on her face cold. "If that's the real reason you trekked all the way up here, you can start back down the mountain right now."

With a gallows humor, he said, "You see? From now on I'll think right up to this second, wishing I hadn't asked...kicking myself...asking, 'what if' I'd waited until next time."

"Ease your mind," she snapped. "The answer would still be no." She came down the ladder, shoved the quilt into his arms and pushed him out of the room. "Good night." Then, "What is it about you doctors that makes you think you know everything?"

The corner of his mouth twitched. "Arrogance. Do you know a lot of doctors?"

"I'm surroundded by them!" she said closing the door.

Jerry stared at it for several moments before retreating to make up the sofa. This interlude on Talking Rock had been a godsend. He had been worn down; these last few months of his residency were spiking his energy. He glanced once more toward Calico's bedroom. *For a fact*, he thought, *a man has to learn to live with regret.*

12

SHE STACKED BREAKFAST DISHES on the wooden drain-board. Jerry Bass lay sleeping on the sofa, snoring in little gasps. Only Christian had eaten. Calico had no appetite for food; she fed herself on thoughts of Irish McCaulley, some of which she could barely endure, so that everything inside her was at sixes and sevens.

It was a somnolent autumn morning and bitter cold, yet there was no wind, the sun shining so still she could see dust motes in the air through which her grandfather hobbled down the path out back. He was subdued this morning, as if his revelations of the night before weighed heavily on his shoulders. That was another of the things that badgered her. Christian was alert, himself, with no sign of vagueness. Only his usual contentiousness was missing. He had stared at Jerry's sleeping form this morning before moving to the table.

"Do you like that young man?" He had looked embarrassed.

"Don't get ideas, grampa. He's nice, but not special to me."

"You'll be all alone up here when I die."

She slid eggs from the frying pan onto his plate. "I never feel alone on the mountain. And you're not going to die. So hush." He ate mechanically, his eyes clouded, as if taking nourishment was part of a plan, a strategy that he had mapped out.

Calico sighed heavily as Christian disappeared around the bend in the path, and removed the apron she wore, running her hands down her sides. The gesture was an old habit, one that wore the ribs on her brown cord slacks so that the cloth over her hips was as threadbare as that at her knees. She wrung out dishcloths and took them to hang on the line on the back porch.

It was then she heard the dog bark, saw the chickens scattering with flapping wings and cacophonous squawking as it raced through their midst. At about the same time Irish came striding into the clearing.

She could not take her eyes from him, yet she made no effort to speak. It was enough that he had returned. He wore a black turtleneck sweater beneath a suede coat and slacks colored gray, clothes that made him attractive with a natural elegance, and yet his presence fit the wildness of the mountain. He called Sam to heel, then spying her through the screen, detoured to the porch.

"Hello." His breath misted like fog in the cold air.

She wanted to welcome him, say all the right things, but the ache in her was patent. She blurted. "I want to know all about Belle." It was impossible for her to shape the word wife. "Why a divorce in the first place?"

He ignored her outburst. "Invite me in for coffee, say hello, say you're glad to see me."

She held open the screen for him, leading the way into the cabin, through the thick outer door into the warmth the wood burning stove was putting out. "Come in for coffe, and hello," she repeated in a tone tinctured with annoyance. He lifted one dark eyebrow as he took a seat at the table while she poured coffee and sat opposite him. "Well?"

He was laughing, smiling, happy. "Are you wondering what's so wrong with me that another woman won't have me?"

"You're always mocking me," she said to his teasing tone. "I know Belle wants you. I remember the elegant way she walked in and possessed you."

His ire began to sputter. "Possessed? Belle doesn't possess me, I'm my own man. No one possesses me."

She tossed him an uneasy glance. "I want to believe you, but I can't. I have to know about Belle. I don't want to pursue this any more than you say you do, but I—what scandal keeps you from a divorce?"

Irish snorted. "Scandal! Belle's father, old Amos himself, sailed into the family bank on the tail of a scandal when his cousin lifted a few of the bank's receipts. His Uncle Drew was the president then, and when Drew's son absconded with the money, Drew called in Amos, who, I'm told, was only too happy to leap into the vacancy. That was before my time, but I can assure you, Belle's family thrives on scandals, audits, and gossip. They have nothing to do with Belle's current perverseness. No, she's embarrassed herself somewhere and needs a place to run to. This isn't the first time."

"Are you going to take her back? Have you?"

"Calico, I swear if somebody died, you'd ask them if they were really dead," he sighed, exasperated. "The answer is no." He wished there was some way to deflect the bent of this conversation. Some things were terribly private, but he could see by the look on Calico's face, she wasn't going to be put off. "Look, I told you before what Belle is like. She's...I'm just not about to accept the leftovers in life. I'm tired of them." His voice dropped to a velvet smoothness as he reached for her.

Calico drew back. "Don't touch me!"

"Don't touch you?" He was incredulous. "*Don't touch you*? It's all I've been thinking about for days. I want to hold you, make love to you, make you love me. How long do you expect me to be able to keep this table between us?'' His eyes burned, caressing her.

I'm a second, a leftover, she thought, *so I guess it'll stay between us forever.* ''You're going to abandon me,'' she said, her voice so flat, so dead, he could only stare at her with a helpless rage.

''I haven't done anything to make you think that,'' he protested. ''Not a thing. You walked out on *me* in Atlanta. I've been caught up in business, the ceremony to accept that award, seeing attorneys to iron out licensing my lab, setting up accounts. If you had a telephone...look, I have some great news...'' He moved around the table and stood over her, becoming passionate, trembling with savage longing. ''For God's sake, let me kiss you, let me hold you...''

Jerry raised up on the sofa, hair tousled, quilts rustling, and looked their way. ''Er...better not get carried away, you're not alone,'' he said with apologetic embarrassment, his cheeks reddened.

Irish spun on his heels, blood rising in his face, glancing from Jerry Bass to Calico and back at Jerry. ''Who in the hell are you?''

''Dr. Gerald Bass—Emory,'' he said, coming to his feet. He slept in worn hospital greens that gave him a boyish air, but they lent authority to his reply. ''And you?''

''Dr. Nathan McCaulley,'' Irish spat, his pride wrapped in cold fury.

Jerry's sleep-ridden eyes widened. ''*The* Dr. McCaulley?''

Irish didn't deign to answer. He grabbed Calico's hand, pulling her out of the chair and drew her outside into the cold for privacy. ''Who is he?'' he demanded. ''What's he doing here? Are you sleeping with him?''

She noted the thread of jealousy in his voice, recognizing the danger of it. ''Did you find him in my bed?'' she snapped, withdrawing her hand. She was mortified that he should ask her such a question. "Who's bed has Belle been sleeping in?"

The muscles in his lean jaw throbbed. "Don't try twisting me, Calico. I'm warning you—"

"What's going on here?" Christian said, approaching them.

"Grampa! I didn't hear you come up. This is Irish McCaulley. He's a friend of Phillip Braeswood's and the man I pulled from the river. He was here when you collapsed."

"Sir," Irish said, swiftly curbing his anger.

Christian became deadly still, his mouth set like iron, but his gaze roamed over Irish and met the younger man's eyes. Then slowly, dreamlike, he shifted all his weight to his crutches. His mind seemed to travel elsewhere. "Now I see why—"

Christian stopped abruptly in midsentence, turning to Calico. "I'll be in the shed if you want me. Tell Jerry when he wakes." He gave Irish one last penetrating glance before hobbling off, his shoulders hunched and bent. He had been taciturn and short, not even casually attempting a greeting to Irish. Calico felt the urge to apologize.

"He didn't mean to be rude...he's.... So many years in prison left him wary and suspicious. Sometimes it seeps through."

"I understand," Irish told her, unconcerned. "Look, can we stop this haggling? I've missed you. I'm going to get those divorce papers filed, somehow. Trust me."

The emotions in Calico that had receded at Christian's interruption erupted again. "Trust you? Over God? You're both men, aren't you? And He's already failed me once." Calico did not have on her long underwear, and the blue flannel shirt she wore was doing little to keep out the cold. She made a move toward the inside warmth of the cabin.

"Wait," Irish ordered. "The first time we made love, you called it destiny. Why are you turning me away now? Are we no longer destined?" The desire in him raged, a potent thing, undeniable, unquenchable.

"I made a mistake," Calico replied.

It was a token defense, yet now, Irish did not attempt to breach it. Truth was, his feelings were hurt. He wouldn't admit to it in a thousand years. He was disappointed. He had expected to be welcomed into the warmth of her arms. He was back in the orphanage, a little boy, overlooked, unwanted. He became bellicose. "You know how I feel about you. I'll be on the mountain, at Phillip's place—my place now." The surprise in her eyes pleased him. "I'm building my laboratory up here. If you change your mind, you know where to find me." He slammed off the porch, calling Sam to heel.

Calico opened her mouth to speak, closed it, then tried again. "You can't."

"I can, and I will," he said, stopping to talk over his shoulder. "Phillip's lease is life long, and there are no restrictions."

"You can't have electricity. Grampa won't have it!"

He smiled with a wry twist of his lips. "Can't bring it up from rural electric, but I don't need to. I'm using gas-powered generators. They're far more stable anyway." He sauntered a few more paces toward the pine groves. "You know where I'll be, if you want company." It was his parting shot. Calico watched until he and the dog disappeared into the forest.

"Is it safe to come out and wash up now?" Jerry asked, poking his head around the door.

"Plenty safe," Calico muttered abrasively. "Grampa's in the shed. He wants to see you."

"You know I'm leaving this afternoon. I have to be back at the hospital for the graveyard shift. Will you

give me a lift to the highway?" When she didn't
answer right away, Jerry attempted small talk. "Funny thing, running into Dr. McCaulley up here on
Talking Rock. Are you two old friends?"

"We're not friends at all," she retorted, responding
to his conversational lure. "He's building his laboratory up here."

Jerry Bass would like to have pursued this line of
talk. That McCaulley had left Bateman Medical to set
up his own lab was medical news, but Calico's eyelids
dipped and the contours of her angular face shifted.
She had closed him out.

"I'll be close by, just holler up when you're ready to
leave." She was filled with the compulsion to visit the
scree, to talk out the confusion in her mind with her
mother, her grandmother. If they could answer, what
would they say to her now that she had fallen in love
with a married man?

13

THERE WAS NO STOPPING IRISH from building his laboratory on Talking Rock. Astonishingly, Christian voiced
no objection. In fact, he seemed to take an avid interest in the construction as the building went up,
though he remained curiously remote from Irish
McCaulley.

While winter was deadheading in on the mountain,
a building going up meant work, and in Appalachia
work was always welcome. Even old Jebediah, with
his exquisite woodworking skills, had been courted.
He was creating some specially-designed shelves and
cabinets for the lab and the wire-and-wooden cages
that would house the test animals kept there. Car-
penters, stonemasons, roofers and even a road builder
were kept busy on the other side of Talking Rock.

Calico couldn't get away from it—no matter where
she went the sounds of sawing, hammering, men's
shouts reached her ears. A portable generator gave
rise to things to come. It kept power tools humming
and buzzing. Irish's cabin had been wired. He had a
refrigerator, electric lamps, and had even installed an
electric toilet.

Now that Jebediah was working on Talking Rock,
Winnie came up almost every day, preparing lunch
with foodstuffs brought from home. Calico didn't object because with Winnie to keep Christian company,
she was free to roam and prospect and pan. A path
was worn between their cabin and that of Irish's by
Jebediah as he padded between the two. Each day that

he arrived for lunch, he began spouting praise for Irish before he had his muffler unwound from his neck. It was McCaulley this or McCaulley that, or that young scientist....

"He's not young," Calico snapped when she'd had her fill.

"Forty-two's young to me," Jebediah said, eyeing her. "Now in a woman, that's another matter. Thirty is long in the tooth...."

His caustic barb was not well-taken and she stomped from the room.

Irish did not return to her side of the mountain, nor had he sent her a message. She knew he was waiting, and she determined she could be as stubborn as he was, but she longed to get a glimpse of him. When she was out, bundled against the cold, she stealthily made her way to a small rise, thick with pine, that gave her a close vantage point.

She discovered that the laboratory was Irish's dream and he did more than just direct the builders, he helped. She watched as boards leaped at him, hitting his ankles and shins. Nails bent and flew everywhere except into wood, and hammers seemed to find his fingers with appalling regularity. He had developed a vocabulary of the most expressive oaths—and the men working for him loved it. They laughed, but leaped to his side at every misadventure.

The mountain was no longer Calico's private refuge. For the first time she felt an unaccustomed strangeness. She was feeling left out.

Sometimes as she watched the building going up, she would catch a flash of Irish as he stood back to survey the timbers and there would cross his face an expression of melancholy, and she would be reminded of the tattered note he'd left on the cabin door. He must've left a mile of notes behind him in his lifetime, she would think. It was at those times that her determination faltered, and when she felt her loneliness so keenly. It took whatever pride she could muster to turn away.

THE DAY BEFORE THANKSGIVING Jebediah and Winnie arrived at the cabin earlier than usual. Winnie collared Calico to help unload boxes of food from the pickup. There were a leg of smoked venison, a pepper-cured ham, a baking hen, cake and pie makings, sweet yams and new potatoes. Onions, olives and nuts.

Calico gazed at all the food piled high on the table and the wooden drainboards. "All this for Thanksgiving dinner, Winnie? There's only the four of us, and Jerry Bass, if he makes it."

Winnie repinned her slipping bun, in disarray from charging in and out of the cabin so hurriedly, then warmed her hands at the stove. "Be more than just us," she said spritely. "The Professor," she went on, using her pet name for Irish, "was upset because he got a note that Phillip Braeswood is coming up for the holidays, bringing his wife and baby. Jebediah asked them over here, 'cause the professor's not set up to do no great amount of cooking. Place is in a mess what with all the men trotting in and out."

"But...but..." Calico said, losing her poise.

"No buts about it. The professor was mightily relieved."

"Irish McCaulley is actually coming—here?" Calico's voice lifted with an undercurrent of trepidation.

Winnie removed her heavy overcoat, hung it on a peg by the back door and tied an apron over her housedress. She shot a sly glance at Calico. "It's amazing to me how you young folks think we oldsters walk around with blinders on. Everybody knows you have a crush on that man and that you've had a spat. Be a good opportunity for you all to patch things up. The professor would 'a come before now, he's so sick of his own cooking, but he wasn't up to how you'd take it."

"He's a married man," Calico stated, her voice trembling a little.

For a moment Winnie was silent, then she pursed her lips, drawing all her wrinkles in about her mouth. "Married is as married does. God works in mysterious ways, it ain't for us to figure." She began sorting the foodstuffs. "I'll take your help in peeling onions, potatoes, and you can bone this fryer; I'll need the meat for giblet gravy."

"Later," Calico said, struggling to throw off the inertia that had come over her. She was remembering how Irish clashed with Jerry. It would be wonderful to see Irish again, be in the same room with him, talk with him, yet she dreaded the confrontation that might ensue between the two doctors. She must, she decided, talk to Irish. Today.

She dressed warmly, for the weather had a sure sting, a dampness coming on. The fine rift of bitterly cold but sun-drenched days were coming to an end. Before she could get out the door, Christian called her to his side where he sat on the sofa.

"I've been meaning to talk to you," he said.

"What about, grampa?" She was impatient, anxious to set out across the mountain before she lost her bravado. A warning bell went off in her head when she found herself beset by her grandfather's intense stare. He spoke without preamble.

"I never felt like I was banished to hell for being instrumental in Vernon's death."

"You don't have to explain anything to me," she cautioned soothingly, feeling a sense of apprehension worming its way up her spine. He might be on the verge of another black spell. He hadn't had one since before Jerry came, but of late, Christian had often seemed lost in thought, as if he was engaged in some ponderous debate.

"Let me talk," he ordered, brushing aside her words carelessly. Calico shrugged out of her sheepskin coat and sat down, burying a sigh. "This other—" Christian began, then stopped short and took up his thought elsewhere. "God is looking over my shoulder, punishing me, dredging it up, making me see myself. I'm an old man, not even a *nice* old man—"

"Yes you are, grampa, and I love you just the way you are."

"You don't know no better," he growled. "I'm full of old hates, old guilts. I want to have peace now, be shed of it."

Calico's eyes widened, catching the flickering gold of flames as they crackled in the hearth. "Shed of what? You raised me. Am I so worthless?"

His head shot up, his aged face paling because she mistook his meaning. "You! You've been my life, but I've done you wrong, too, keeping you up here on this desolate mountain with me."

"Desolate? Grampa, I love being here, the mountain has given me everything, food, a livelihood, shelter...and you, too." *And Irish McCaulley,* but for the moment her mind buckled away from that.

"The mountain's just took from me—Lucy, McKenzie, Ellen and now you."

"Grampa!" she protested. "Do you see me going anywhere? I'm here and I'm not leaving. Your mind's all twisted up somehow."

He shook his head while digging around in his pocket for pipe and tobacco pouch. "I know all of your moods, Calico. I know when you're angry, when you're happy, when you're not and in between, but I don't know this mood you're in now." He turned on her with a strange glint in his watery blue eyes. "This man, Irish McCaulley, when his name's mentioned your face lights up, and Jeb's seen you lurking around the laboratory. Don't deny it," he said, putting off her protests. "That don't matter to me. One thing I've got to know—is McCaulley special to you? Do you like him."

Calico concentrated on picking a loose thread from her cords. "I might."

"Either you do or you don't. Tell me!"

"I do." Her hand went to her throat to stop other words from gushing out.

With thick fingers that were less than steady, Christian began to pack his pipe. "I just wanted to be sure," he murmured. "He's what my mission is; I know it, sure as I'm sitting here talking to you."

"Your mission?" She was mystified, trying desperately to digest what he was saying. "How?"

"The telling of it is for him alone, when I'm ready." Christian's translucent eyes turned cold. "You're not to mention a word of this." He shot a warning glance toward Winnie at the sink. "To anyone."

"But—"

"Swear!" he growled, and raised himself painfully to his feet. "Swear on your mother's grave."

"I—I swear," said Calico, utterly confused. The urge to see Irish waned a little, yet she understood, or thought she understood, that their fates were woven together. Something in her grandfather's past linked them. She shrank from the idea that whatever it was would part them, not bring them together. Her own brutal secret rose to the surface of her mind.

THERE WAS NO SAMENESS about the mountain. Its contours changed season by season as did its colors. Rocks fell, trees grew taller or were bent by the wind; flowers sprouted and faded, cudzu vines floated toward the sky, swaying in treetops. The thick gray vines were leafless, looking like Medusa's hair, grasping and writhing as they tried to snag a low-flying

cloud. Calico noticed nothing of this. She was re-
hearsing in her mind what she would say to Irish as
she followed the newly made path.

Hammer thuds and the buzzing of saws intensified
as she drew nearer the clearing in which the lab was
being built alongside the original cabin. She stepped
from the thicket of trees and her eyes picked out Irish
amoung his workers, on the roof swabbing tar before
laying shingles.

She lifted her foot to step forward and found herself, lightninglike, being propelled backward into the
treeline. "Wha—" she shouted, her mind racing,
wondering if she had tumbled into the path of a bear
seeking a den. She could feel the grip on her collar
from the back, pulling her, jerking, the force yanking
a button to the hollow in her neck, cutting off her air.
She flailed her arms, losing her balance, struggling
violently, then unexpectedly she was free, lying on
her back in rotting pine straw, eyes closed, gasping for
breath.

"Never expected you to come right down that
path," Judalon Tarrant said, leering as he hunched
over her. "You been sneaking around on that hill over
yonder."

Her eyes flew open. "You low life!" she ground out,
the words rasping painfully in her throat. She moved
to a sitting position, keeping a wary eye on the lum-
bering man, then gained her feet.

The leer turned into a grin. "Quit pretending you
don't like me. I seen you watching me working on
this place."

"Like you?" she flung at him scornfully. "Never in
a million years could I come close to liking you, Judalon. I've never come here to watch you. I didn't even
know you'd been hired. If I had, I would've seen you
run off this mountain!"

He put out a hand to touch her and with her fist,

Calico deflected it. Judalon's face contorted with angry surprise. "That ain't no way to treat me." He lunged, grabbing her, twisting her arm behind her back, pressing himself against her. "I ain't had a woman in a long time. Jobeth won't let me near her, her time's so close!" His breath was foul in her face; Calico turned away in disgust, gasping at the pain in her arm.

"Come on, hold still. This ain't no way to treat a man." He shoved her arm high up her back until excruciating pain shot through her.

"I think it might be the way to treat a bully, though," Irish said with deceptive calmness and drove his fist into the side of Judalon's head. Calico was loose in that instant with Judalon not down, but shaking his large head as if to clear it of swirling lights.

"You ain't got no right to interfere here," he protested weakly.

"See the foreman, Judalon, and collect your wages," said Irish coldly. "If I find you around here again, I'll have the sheriff after you for trespassing."

Judalon's dark eyes bore into Calico. "You done this...cause a man to git fired when's he got a family to feed."

Irish stepped between them and said bluntly. "I hired you on because your wife is Calico's friend. You haven't earned a tenth of what you've been paid—now clear out." The tone of his voice had a dangerous edge. Judalon backed up, then turned and made off to the foreman's shack.

"That's not the kind of reception I'd planned just in case you came to see me," Irish said, turning to Calico. There was something strange, a sign he couldn't read reflected in her eyes. "Did he hurt you?"

"I'm fine, he just took me off guard." Her legs were trembling, so she leaned casually against the nearest tree. Irish took her hands in a vicelike grip and the current that shot into her was monumental. Every word she had planned to say slipped off into space like an aberrant missile. He smelled of hot tar and soap and male sweat, and the cold had put red into his cheeks that was appealing.

"Come down to the cabin with me. I'll make us some coffee. I've become almost expert on that tin stove. You can tell me what you've been up to...."

Reluctantly she pulled her hands from his. "I can't. Winnie expects me back to help her."

"Why did you come then; just out for a stroll?" A vestige of irony was in his voice.

"I came to tell you that Dr. Bass—Jerry—is probably coming to Thanksgiving dinner tomorrow. You were rude to him last time. I—I don't want there to be any trouble."

"I see." His tone was gritty. "I'm supposed to watch him sniff around you and do nothing, is that it? Am I to believe he hasn't made a pass at you?"

Calico hesitated for just a breath, that internal second that ticks by when deciding how much of a truth to tell. Irish drove his scraped and tar-spattered hands into his pockets. "Maybe I shouldn't have busted in on you and Judalon," he said testily.

Despite the lopsided manner in which her stocking cap sat on her head and that her braid was caught with dead straw, Calico's dignity was intact. She moved forward, standing proudly erect, her eyes steely and remaining on his face. "I'm glad you did, but Jerry *is* something that neither you or Judalon Tarrant can lay a claim to."

"Oh, and what would that be?"

"Jerry Bass is single." She turned on her heel and sped down the path, away from Irish, rubbing her arm, angry with herself, with Irish, and hating Judalon with a fervor that crept into her soul.

SINGLE! Bleakly Irish watched Calico merge into the pine and fir trees that appeared feathery in the forest gloom. He massaged his knuckles, stinging from the blow he had given to the side of Judalon's head. The bully. Showed his true colors by backing off at the first sign of strength. But Judalon was only a momentary irritant. Irish's mind went back to a conversation he'd had with Phillip.

"I've got to get out from under Belle. I'm going to file for divorce myself, here in Atlanta."

"Can't you wait?" Phillip had pleaded grimly. "Just until the lab is built, until you've received a grant or two?"

"I don't want to wait. I thought I was already free of her. It churns my gut to know I'm not, and there are others to consider." He was thinking of Calico, seeing himself fitted between her thighs, his hand stroking her silken skin, her quicksilver eyes somber with desire—wanting him, needing him, as much as he needed her.

"Irish. Listen. I sympathize with you, but you're already a maverick. I hate to say it, but Belle is vitriolic. You know it and I know it. She'll get nasty. She'll try to discredit your work. You know how delicately balanced egos and reputations are in medicine. Foundations don't like scandal."

"What can Belle do?" Irish retorted, full of skepticism. "Nothing."

"Nothing? My friend, she's been frothing at the mouth since walking in on you and Calico Jones. And she had lunch one day with Gerald Vincent. I've no doubt they're cooking up something between them. He's been fired from Bateman, you know. You're grist in his craw. He had an ultimatum—get you back on the staff at Bateman or pack his bags...."

Irish raised an eyebrow in surprise. "I had no idea, but it couldn't have happened to a more deserving—"

"That's beside the point if he and Belle conspire together to spread rumors," interrupted Phillip impatiently. "It could hurt you—and us, your investors. We're not being selfish. We want you to succeed. All I'm asking is for you to wait—be patient...."

"It's not one of my virtues."

"Look, I'll drive up to Talking Rock for Thanksgiving with Ginny and Sarah. We'll talk more then. A week from now—can you hold off until then? Maybe something will break in our...your favor."

A week. It had come and gone. Irish glanced down at his scraped knuckles. Determination swelled within him. Monday he was driving into Atlanta and seeing a lawyer—a divorce lawyer. Calico was in his blood. If he didn't have her soon, he wouldn't be fit to work, to concentrate, to pull together all the interminable details setting up the laboratory required. Slowly, thoughtfully, Irish turned back to the clearing. The sharp acrid smell of hot tar lay heavy in the chill air as he strode purposefully to take his place among his men.

At noon he had the foreman, Willie Boles, who was called Cups for no fathomable reason he could ascertain, pay off the men, a half-dozen locals, including Jebediah, for the holidays. "Remind everyone we start work again eight in the morning, Friday," he said. "And Cups, don't forget to give out those certificates for turkeys at Big Star."

"Naw, I won't," Cups replied. "The men been anticipatin' em."

Irish had a thought. "Did you give Tarrant one when you paid him off?"

Cups shook his head, moving his chew of tobacco from one side of his jaw to the other. "Naw. He ain't even come close to earning the money you paid him."

Recalling Jobeth and the two youngsters he'd met, Irish felt a pang of guilt. It didn't seem right to deprive

them because of Judalon's crass and lazy behavior.
"Do you know where Tarrant lives? Could you pick
up a turkey and take it to his wife?"

Cups spit a stream of tobacco expertly. "My wife'll
do it. I'm not up to women's errands."

"Good enough," Irish said, wondering if he would
ever come to understand the particular code and customs by which these mountain people lived.

CALICO PEELED AND CUT ONIONS until they made her cry.
The opportunity was too good to pass up. She shed a
few real tears of self-pity until a sob broke from her
throat that made Winnie spin around and loosened
her chignon. "Them's the most powerful onions I
ever saw," she observed suspiciously.

"They are, aren't they?" Calico sniffed.

Winnie bustled about the sink, the stove and the
table like a brisk north wind. "Here, rub these apples
with lard, then sprinkle 'em down with nutmeg and
poke these cloves into 'em. I'll set 'em to baking, give
us a holiday aroma about this place." The offensive
onions were whisked into a skillet, bubbling with
butter. After a few minutes Winnie suddenly turned
from the stove. "I don't know what all this foolish-
ness is about, Calico... or why you're carrying on so,
but you... you ought to get married." She stared at
Calico defiantly, her old face held stiffly, ready to retreat behind God, the devil, or whomever was handy,
depending on Calico's reaction.

Calico bolted up. "I only want to marry whom *I
want* to marry!"

Winnie's eyes widened in surprised understanding. "It's about time you done picked him out."
There was a dreadful look on Calico's face, and Winnie was torn between saying something soothing and
her usual complaining. It mixed her up. "We can
never be certain of the future, sometimes not even

the next minute—happens it might get snatched away. Then again, God dumps somethin' good right into our laps."

"Not in mine, he doesn't," said Calico acidly.

"You blaspheme, Calico Jones. It ain't fittin'!"

IT WAS ONLY WHEN HE WAS LYING IN BED, reviewing his day, sorting it into various pieces, that Irish thought to probe Judalon Tarrant's actions. What had the man been up to, attacking Calico like that? Stealing a kiss? He should have hit the man harder, Irish thought with a fiery twinge of jealousy. His mind harked back to the day Judalon had come to pick up his boys after spending the night in jail. The hostility projected by Calico had been thick in the air. A long-standing feud, mountain fashion? Perhaps Judalon had dipped that lovely copper braid in an inkwell when they had been children. If Calico wasn't involved, Irish decided he would be amused.

Jobeth, Judalon, Winnie, Jebediah and, of course, her grandfather—these were people Calico had known all of her life. The only person he had known a lifetime was Sister Antonio. It made him sad. Apart from her, there wasn't a single person from the orphanage with whom he was still acquainted—whether friend or enemy. Once a child had been adopted, a continuing relationship had been forbidden, so he never had known what had happened to the adopted children he'd played with or fought with as a youngster.

For the first time in months Irish had the old dream of taking his scalpel to himself to look inside.

14

DINNER WAS TO BE AT ONE-THIRTY.

Calico thought the hands on the clock nestled among the books on the shelf near the fireplace were taking too long to move from one second to the next, from one minute to the next—hours were nonexistent. "You're going to break that clock if you keep shaking it like that," Winnie admonished irritably. "Put on an apron and punch this bread down, then shape it into loaves and get it in the oven. I need help. It ain't like I'm in my own kitchen."

Calico sighed. It was easier to endure than protest. For the first time in her memory, Thanksgiving was being celebrated on Talking Rock. In the past all holidays had been spent at the foot of the mountain. She desperately wanted things to run smoothly, yet there was an underlying tension in the air. Jebediah was unusually quiet, Winnie unusually vinegarish and her grandfather...he was behaving like a man about to evict his soul. As for her own mind...it was filled with images of Irish McCaulley.

"Quit pounding on that dough like you was pulverizing gold rock!" Winnie's voice startled her. "And watch it when you get it in the oven; heat sets to the left. You got to keep turning the pans and don't forget to set a dish of water in the bottom. I don't want crusts like concrete, and brush the tops with egg whites, but don't leave them on the stove, else they'll cook up." Calico expelled another heavy sigh, her carefully masked emotions rising to the surface.

"Yes, Winnie; no, Winnie," she muttered beneath her breath.

"You sassin' me?" Winnie spat contrarily. Her chief aim in life that day was to prepare food. Professor McCaulley was now her husband's boss. Everything had to be just so.

"Would you listen if I were?" Calico returned perversely.

"Lordy! No wonder Christian spends so much time on my back porch and took to drink like he has," the old woman sniffed. "And all this time I've been afeelin' for you." She fixed Calico with a stern eye. "You just set the name to the man you want to marry and I'll help you along. Wait too much longer and you ain't going to be fit to tote off to no marriage bed. You have a diseased tongue, Calico Jones. It comes from living up here on this wild mountain, raised by a man who ain't got sense God gave to Adam, and that was little enough!"

"I thought grampa raised me the way you told him to," Calico replied blandly.

"Showed him how to change a diaper once, and ain't got in a word since. Shows too. Now get outta my way. Go see if those chickens laid any eggs what ain't froze up. We're running low."

Calico grabbed up a jacket off a peg and made her escape. The weather was half-sunny, darkening at moments as clouds darted in front of the sun, and the air was crisply cold. She skirted the work shed, where her grandfather and Jebediah were warming themselves by a fire built in an old metal drum. They had had the sense to get out of Winnie's way right after breakfast.

She was returning to the cabin with an apron full of brown-speckled eggs when a car door slammed. Irish! But one-thirty was hours away. No matter, the mountain was working its magic. She raced around the side of the house, hiding her disappointment as Jerry Bass emerged from a small red Volvo. He was grinning. "I could smell the aroma of baked ham and turkey halfway down the road. My mouth's watering."

"Where'd you get the car?" she asked. There was something about Jerry that prompted conversations to continue regardless of the pause between them... in minutes or weeks. A quality, she surmised, that would stand him in good stead in his line of work.

"Dr. Marcavitch loaned it to me. It's his wife's."

"That stern-faced arrogant old man?" she queried in surprise. "I thought he didn't like you."

"Oh, he adores me. I'm the only resident who stands up to him." Jerry looked at her approvingly. She was wearing a rust-colored skirt with a plaid blouse, stockings and penny loafers. Neither the jacket nor the apron full of eggs could hide her trim attractive look, and the chill air put red into her cheeks. "Are you all decked out for me?" he asked.

Calico brushed his compliment aside, saying firmly, "Thanksgiving." She wasn't going to let Jerry start something when she'd already put Irish on notice of his manners. "You're not the only company we're having."

"Oh? Are you sure I won't be intruding?"

"Positive," she replied. "It's only Irish McCaulley and some people we lease land to on the other side of the mountain."

"*Only* Irish McCaulley." Jerry assumed an expression of impassivity. "I'll bet a duck you manage to bring him down a notch or two."

The smile she was wearing collapsed. "What's that supposed to mean?"

"Don't you know he's turned the medical community on its collective ear? Leaving Bateman, setting up his lab—"

"So?"

Jerry shook his head, grinning. "So, I give up, you're not one to be awed. Don't know how I could forget it. Tell me about your grandfather. How is he?"

"My hands are getting cold. Let's go inside," she said brusquely.

Jerry's eyes narrowed. "Wait a minute. You're not telling me something. What is it?"

Calico hesitated, her gaze sweeping out over the mountain, taking in the evergreens that stood like lonely sentinels amid winter-bare oak and poplar. Her scrutiny stopped at the scree and the even lonelier graves. "I can't put it into words exactly...sometimes I think I'm to blame for the way grampa is—so morose at times. He's taken care of me since I was a baby. I've never really thought about what it cost him in his independence and freedom. When I look back on it now, he was always here—always...." She shivered, her voice trailing off, caught by the wind as it slid down the sluice. "Grampa says he knows what his mission is."

"And?"

"Nothing. I can't say more because he made me swear not to."

Jerry's hands hung limply at his side for a moment, then he clapped them together. "I think maybe that's good news," he said slowly.

"How can it be good?" A keen sense of uneasiness overwhelmed her; the feeling that whenever she anticipated good, it was undone by bad. When she'd been in the second grade, she'd been invited to a birthday party she was hungering to attend. She'd come down with measles and couldn't go. When she was fourteen, she had entered a clogging contest, made it to the finals, then sprained an ankle. Just when she had thought they were going to get electricity, a truck fell in a hole and Christian changed his mind. The mountain gave her Irish McCaulley, and

afterward she discovered he had a wife. And even if
there was no wife, he didn't want seconds. No good
could come from her grandfather's mission. He was
just an old man, trying to erase his bitterness. Still,
she loved him, and didn't want him to come to any
harm.

"Good," Jerry was saying, "because he's thought
about it, let it rattle around in his head. Don't you
see? He's beginning to accept whatever it is that's in
his past." There was a thread of excitement in his
voice.

"But there's no way—" Calico stopped abruptly.
She couldn't break an oath taken on her mother's
grave. "Come on, I'll introduce you to Winnie and
Jebediah. Winnie'll be screaming like a bee-stung
dervish if I don't get her these eggs."

"Pray heaven!" Winnie cried, snatching off her
stained and wrinkled apron. "Company ain't suppose
to arrive afore one-thirty."

"I'm not company, " Jerry said, smiling ruefully.
"I'm just a country boy myself. Took Calico up on her
invitation to dinner just so I could get some home
cooking."

"That the truth?" Winnie asked, eyeing him skepti-
cally.

"Cross my heart," Jerry declared.

Winnie smiled slyly. "Fire box is low," she said,
and put him to work chopping wood. Later she
cornered him to grate bar chocolate, butterscotch
chips and pecans for a better-than-sex cake.

"Better than sex, Mrs. Bascomb? You've got to be
putting me on."

For the first time in forty years, a rosy hue swept up
Winnie's cheeks. "You can put yourself in mortal
danger, talking like that," she warned him sharply.
She turned away from him, presenting her thin rigid

back, but still, she seemed to know exactly the moment he began to dip into the batter by the spoonfuls. "Out to the work shed with you!" she announced, snatching the bowl.

Calico smiled. It was heaven or hell with Winnie and nothing in between.

At one-thirty Calico was sitting at her desk, pretending to be absorbed in rock samples. Behind her, every lamp in the cabin was lighted, a fire blazed in the grate, around which extra chairs had been grouped. The table was set with her best dishes and real silver. None matched, but the setting had an elegance all its own. A makeshift sideboard—planks laid across two old sawhouses—was laden with food. Pickles, relishes, cakes, sweet-potato pie, sliced venison, baked ham, the turkey Jebediah had brought from Big Star—compliments of Irish—dishes of homemade butter, stuffed eggs, cranberry sauces and a jar of honey flecked with comb; all of it covered with a pristine white cloth. Giblet gravy, bread, succotash and cornbread dressing were warming in the pie safe; store-bought ice, cooled beer, wine and soft drinks in a bucket. The crisp, sharp scent of clove-sprigged apples clung to the rafters.

Expectantly, Calico kept lifting her eyes to the forest where an old oak, denuded of foliage, marked the beginning of the path across the mountain. She watched for the dog Sam. He would, she knew, herald the approach of Irish and Phillip and Ginny with their baby, Sarah.

They arrived, instead, by car.

15

THERE WAS A KIND OF SUBDUED PANDEMONIUM in the laughter, hand shaking and greetings as everyone met and mingled on the threshold of the cabin. "Get inside, quick," Winnie cried, usurping hostess duties from Calico. "Heat's going to fly out of the house and it'll be too drafty for a baby."

"I thought you'd walk across the mountain," Calico said to no one in particular, feeling stupid once the words were out of her mouth.

"With Sarah?" proclaimed Ginny. "You don't know what it's like moving anywhere with this kid!" Calico smiled weakly.

From the moment he entered, Irish hovered near her and Calico forgot that he had a wife. She erased all thoughts of being a second, pretending that there had never been a cross word between them. Instinctively, she practiced the provoking art of provocation, a ritual as old as woman herself, so ancient it was bred into the soul of Eve even before she had been formed into flesh. She brushed against Irish, letting her fingers touch his; she rested her hand lightly, as if unconsciously, on his shoulder when stopping to chat near him, and was gratified through it all to feel him stiffen perceptibly. Several minutes passed before they actually spoke to one another.

He had been excessively polite to Jerry Bass. It was a paltry way to begin a skirmish. "Am I being nice enough for you?" he asked mockingly as he followed her to the kitchen.

"Oh, real nice. Did you stop to think that he's a psychiatrist and can see right through you?"

"Then he should recognize jealousy when he sees it," he retorted. "And when it comes to you, I always will be—jealous that is."

The unspoken thought that he was married hung between them.

"I don't like you talking like that," she said smoothly, dipping her hands into the ice bucket to bring up several bottles of beer.

"What was Judalon up to yesterday, anyway?"

Calico stiffened. "Just being a bully like he's always been."

"Are the two of you feuding?" Irish stepped closer, placing his arm about her waist, leaning into her so that she became aware of his spicy fragrance, the tiny streaks of gray at his temples, his hair overlong now and curling against the nape of his neck.

"No...yes. Mind your own business." His lips brushed her ear, making her tremble so that she fumbled about opening the bottles.

"I'm trying to make things right between us," he whispered. "These past weeks have been hell. Being on the same mountain, knowing you were sleeping, eating, wandering around...so close...."

His words thrilled her. So he had suffered, too. "You could've walked over here anytime you wanted—and been welcome."

"A man has his pride."

She angled a glance at his face. "It gets in the way of a lot of things for you, doesn't it? Now let me by, they're waiting on these." She placed the beers on a tray, trying to move past him, but he blocked her way.

"Are you by any chance trying to be deliberately coy? If so, I'll remind you that *you* began all this. You were the one who locked all the doors, you were the one who stood before that fireplace over there and began to undress. You asked me to make love to you. I had no intentions of it, you know."

Her head shot up, eyes flashing like silver streaks, her voice as icy as the wind careening about the cabin. "I didn't know. How could I? You kept on and on, even...even when you knew you had no right! Like now! Are you going to let me serve these drinks or not?" Nothing was going the way she planned or hoped. Her stomach began to twist into knots. Love was a far more painful emotion than hate, it left her confused, drifting into an emotional limbo. Calico felt watched and looking beyond Irish's shoulder, discovered her grandfather staring at them with a burning intensity. She had never felt the lack of her mother, her grandmother more keenly than at that moment. She felt herself wedged between Irish and Christian as tightly as if she'd stumbled and been stuck in a crevasse. "Grampa's staring," she said. "You're making a spectacle...."

Tight lipped, Irish stepped out of her way. "You may think I'll beg, but I won't," he tossed at her softly.

Calico endeavored to ignore him the remainder of the afternoon.

GINNY BRAESWOOD WAS ENTHRALLED with Talking Rock, the cabin, praising the sideboard of food until Winnie beamed and was coaxed to give up old family recipes. Fourteen-month-old Sarah seemed to know exactly what was expected of her. Passed from hand to hand, she cooed, gurgled and smiled, then explored the wide-planked floor under her mother's watchful eyes until she found the wooden box of rock samples beneath Calico's desk. They occupied her throughout dinner.

Avoiding Irish used up a great deal of Calico's willpower and she let her mind wander among the snippets of conversation. "Oh, Sarah was sitting up when she was only five months." "Copper pot, that's the secret to the best home brew. Copper won't kill ya." "I'm a scientist, always was misplaced in teaching." "... the study of our brain and behavior will never be an exacting science." "You can never tell what Calico's up to till she's gone and done it." "... mined that hole for ten hours, pulled twenty ounces of gold, best day I ever had."

Christian was far more loquacious than Calico had ever heard him. He shaped his words slowly, talked of his past, gold finds, his days in medical school, even an anecdote of prison life. At the mention of prison, she came alert, shaking off the lethargy a heavy meal induced, not that she had tasted a single forkful. Christian seemed to be directing most of his conversation toward Irish, being particularly fierce about it, as if he were shedding the outer layers of himself. Jerry Bass had stopped eating to listen, his face thoughtful, eyes questioning. So he had noticed it, too.

As everyone drifted away from the table, the men for smokes, Ginny to feed Sarah, Calico and Winnie began clearing up. "I'll take care of the table and the dishes, Winnie," Calico volunteered. "You visit with Ginny while she feeds Sarah. She wants to hear about your quilting patterns."

"I'll make coffee first," Winnie declared, openly grateful and tired now that the main event was over.

"I'll make the coffee, Mrs. Bascomb," Irish said, sauntering up.

"Oh, professor. You're company, you don't have—"

"I want to," he replied in his most authoritative tone. Winnie was not about to argue with her husband's boss. She shrugged, moving away, but not before she slanted a sharp glance at Calico.

Now it seemed as if their roles were reversed. As Irish made up the coffeepot, pumping water at the sink, stoking up the fire, setting cups and saucers on the table, he brushed past Calico, touching her lightly, deliberately, as she moved around the table too, scraping plates. After a moment he fished in his pockets for a cigarette. He rarely smoked, but the need for one and something to do with his hands prevailed. He inhaled, blowing smoke toward the rafters. "Think you could set aside some of those scraps for Sam? I had to leave him locked up today. He didn't like it."

Calico nodded, saying nothing, unsure exactly of his strategy.

"Been gold hunting lately?" he asked quite pleasantly.

"Some," she replied absently, her mind preoccupied by his nearness.

"Finding any?"

"A little."

"Like me?"

"A little—no!" *Sneaky!* she thought, and kept stacking dishes, her eyes cast down, but watching his feet to see if he moved toward her.

"I have a refrigerator now, and ice cubes. You're welcome to borrow a tray anytime—say tonight? After everyone's gone home."

She laughed then, and looked at him. "Food mellows you, does it? Happens we have ice today."

The teasing in his voice suddenly went flat. "That's about as close as I'm going to come to asking you." He leaned against the sinks a moment longer, looking at her, his face an impenetrable mask, then without another word, he went to join the men.

Calico watched him go with mixed emotions; an unbearable sense of want, needing him to touch her, and apprehension that the mountain was too full of humans, destroying her peace, her privacy. If only she could escape for a moment, visit the scree, have one of her long silent talks with her mother. Did all women suffer so?

"More company coming," called Winnie from her perch by the window, where she was rocking Sarah while Ginny puffed on a forbidden cigarette. "Looks like Jobeth and her brood. Lordy, yes. All six of them boys crowded into the cab. Mashed like sardines looks like from here."

Just what she needed, Calico thought ironically. On top of everything else, Jobeth and her rowdy boys. But the boys weren't rowdy today. Far from it. They were positively solemn, the younger boys, Mikie and Rafe, showing evidence of tears, as did Jobeth. Her eyes were red, and her hair, always difficult to manage, was flying in a dozen different directions. A brown gabardine coat hung limply about the ample body, impossible to button against the cold over her swollen belly.

"You haven't see Judalon, have you?" Jobeth gushed anxiously the moment they were all ushered inside. She took everyone in with a single glance, wringing her hands. "Have you? Has anybody?"

"Come sit down," Calico said, urging Jobeth to the sofa. "You boys, too. But at the table. Gabe, you know how to work the stove. Stir up some milk and make cocoa—"

"There's cake. I'll get—" Winnie began.

"Wait a minute," interrupted Calico, mindful now of her duties as a hostess. "Ginny, Phillip, this is Jobeth Tarrant, a friend of mine and her boys. That's Gabe, Rafe, Mikie, Frank...."

"All named after saints and angels," Winnie injected. "Which they ain't. Seems to me they must be sick today. What's up with you scoundrels?"

"We ain't seen our pa. He didn't come home from work yesterday," said Rafe, eyeing his mother. Calico exchanged a glance with Irish, as if to say, you saw him last, say something. But Irish remained silent, observant. Ginny volunteered to help get the cocoa, and the children reluctantly left their mother's side and trooped to the table.

Jobeth was now crying softly. "Judalon ain't never missed no holiday—ever—or the boys birthdays or a birthing . . . he's good about that, when he ain't—" She stopped the litany suddenly.

"In jail, down to Gainsville, most likely," said Christian.

"He ain't." Jobeth shook her head. "I—I called. And all the hospitals too. Mrs. Boles, she brought me a turkey, said it come from Dr. McCaulley." She turned to Irish. "I met you once, when I brought Judalon's lunch. Afore that too, but you wasn't awake and up to company."

"I had to let Judalon go yesterday, Mrs. Tarrant," said Irish quietly, almost apologetically. "Maybe he's gone off to find another job."

Phillip and Jerry, feeling themselves not involved with a local issue, moved slightly away and stood with their backsides to the fire.

"He's on this mountain somewhere," Jobeth said adamantly, her voice rising. Then she cut a curiously apprehensive face toward Calico. "Every day he got off work he—he's been looking for that Spanish treasure."

A tiny moan escaped Calico's lips. "Jobeth, I've told you, there's no treasure on Talking Rock. That's rumor, myth, a four-hundred-year-old one at that."

"He's here. I feel it," persisted the distraught woman desperately. "Can't we go looking. I'm afraid he's lying hurt somewhere, one of those old mines mayhap collapsed on him like it did your pa." She began to tremble and fidget and she couldn't keep her hands still.

"What you're feeling maybe is that baby coming on." sputtered Winnie. "Didn't Doc Willis say for you to stay close to home? Ain't you due?"

"Yesterday. That's why I know Judalon ain't up to his tricks. He takes being a daddy real serious." She looked at all the faces around her. "You're all down on Judalon! Especially you, Calico."

Calico blanched at Jobeth's tone of veiled insinuation. "What I think of Judalon—" She stopped her rejoinder, knowing it would sound petty, saying instead, "Jobeth, it's just that you're always having to hunt up Judalon, and he invariably shows up. You're worrying yourself into a snit over nothing. Let me get you some coffee, or a glass of wine."

Having none of it, Jobeth rose awkwardly to her feet, pulling her coat about her as best she could. "I don't want no coffee or wine. I want my husband." She was on the very edge of hysteria, staring at Calico. "You don't have no objections to me and my boys scattering around to look, do you?"

"Oh, sit down," Calico admonished with a suppressed sigh. "You're in no condition to roam about hills and hummocks. If it'll ease your mind, I'll take Gabe and Frank—"

Irish intervened, stepping quickly to her side, his fingers circling her arm. "Excuse us a moment, Mrs. Tarrant," he said. "Phillip and I need a word with Calico."

There was concern in Phillip's usually sparkling eyes, and his brow was wrinkled with a frown when Calico, puzzled, faced him. "Irish told me what happened yesterday, the altercation between himself and Tarrant...do you think your friend would hang around the lab, looking for an opportunity to...well, to wreak vengeance?" He spoke in a low whisper that wouldn't carry to Jobeth.

"Judalon is no friend of mine!" Calico retorted

tersely. "He'll take anything that's not nailed down, but I can't see him holing up over a holiday to...to do spite."

"Why exactly don't you like him? I have the impression you've been feuding for a long time." Irish asked the question with his face carefully devoid of expression.

Calico's mouth went dry. It seemed to her every one of her senses was too alive, too alert. Steps across the wooden floor beat too loudly in her ears, conversation sounded like the caw of crows, her heart thundered in her breast. If she spoke truthfully, she'd lose Irish McCaulley forever. Her chin tilted forward, punctuating her reply. "Judalon's a bully, and I've never liked bullies."

"Is it possible that the man *could* be out there somewhere, lost or hurt in an old mine or a cave?"

Maybe there is a God after all, Calico thought dismally, for he was surely snipping at her personally. "It's possible," she admitted reluctantly and looked at Irish, but his face was unreadable. "I'll go change my clothes," she said with a sigh.

The decision to search for Judalon aroused a chorus of questions and observations and advice. Calico left them to it while she exchanged her skirt and blouse for thick cotton long johns, a pair of tough cords and a flannel shirt. She stuffed her hair beneath a woolen cap and was sliding her knife scabbard onto her belt as she emerged from her room. Jebediah was loading bullets into the breach of her .22 rifle, while Jerry, Irish, Phillip, Gabe and Frank milled about the fireplace. All had donned their coats, hats and gloves. Her grandfather was pulling thick woolen socks over his injured foot.

"You can't go out with us, grampa. You'll never keep up on crutches."

"I told him already," Jebediah said.

"I'm going to sit on the porch, keep a lamp burning. If any of you turns up something, I'll let off the gun to call the rest of you back," he said determinedly.

Calico avoided looking at Jobeth, but she felt the woman's eyes following her. It was menacing somehow, as if Jobeth was no longer her friend, but an enemy.

"What do we look for?" Philip asked as they assembled in the front yard. He was rubbing his hands together with enthusiasm. "I don't wish misfortune on anyone," he said, seeing Calico observe his good humor. "But a good brisk walk after a meal like we just had won't do any harm."

It was decided that they would split into two groups, Jebediah to lead one, Calico the other. They would circle the mountain, working in a grid to check the entrance of each old mine or cave known to them. "The custom for prospectors and miners when working alone has always been to leave behind some piece of personal gear at the mouth of a shaft, so we'll look for that. A hat, a scarf, a handkerchief, a pick." Privately, Calico didn't think Judalon would mark his trail, not while he was sneaking around, *if*, in fact, he was on the mountain. But she kept this observation to herself. She glanced toward the cabin, and seeing Jobeth silhouetted in the window, turned her back. The weather was intemperate, cold and getting colder with the thick promise of rain. Wind blew down the sluice in an eerie discordance. "We'll need flashlights," she said and sent Gabe into the cabin for them.

Gabe and Irish attached themselves to Calico, and at the last moment, Jerry Bass joined them as they left the clearing. The expression on Irish's face hardened. Calico noticed, but said nothing, bracing herself for an outburst. When none came, she hunched down into her sheepskin. They began their search in silence,

each lost in his own thoughts, Calico no different
from the rest. Her spirit was as bleak and gray as the
sky beneath which they tread.

For two hours in the diminishing light, they peered
into cuts, and slicks and old mines, some that were
little more than a gouged-out hole in red clay. They
slipped down gullies, crawled up the other sides,
caught their pants in thorns and brambles. Gabe
shimmied into a hole that showed some recent wear
around its rim and came out of it bent for hell. "Pa
ain't in there," he said, breathing hard, "but the big-
gest damned black bear I ever did see is!"

It was the only moment of levity they shared, and
did little to loosen the tension. "Let's make a pass over
by the lab, just in case," Irish suggested. Calico nodded agreement and led the way. It was dark now, with
no moon rising, no stars, for the heavy clouds hid
them. As always at dusk, the wind picked up, whis-
tling around the trees and seeming to invade every
buttonhole and zipper. They were all shivering from
the cold that seemed to become more intense as the
last light faded and shadows became menacing har-
bors to avoid. There was no sound outside their own
harsh breathing except the wind and the hard rhyth-
mic splashing of the river as it met boulders midstream and flowed on.

Calico topped the rise that led to the clearing first
and the others came abreast. The cabin, the laboratory
and Irish's sports car loomed as barely recognizable
shapes. There was a patch of white fluttering on the
cabin door.

"Looks like somebody's been here," said Jerry Bass.
"That looks like a note pinned to the door. I'll go see."

"No!" Irish roared. "Never mind. I know what the
message is." Jerry Bass stopped in his tracks, discon-
certed, and , after casting a questioning look at Irish,
moved back up the hill. Calico squinted at Irish, not

making out his features in the darkness, but able to note that his entire body had stiffened. With a small shuddering shock, she realized what it must have cost him to have her know about the notes, the bits of directions he always left behind. Jerry Bass, being a psychiatrist, would have a field day with that. Irish, she knew, was probably thinking the same thing.

"It's no use standing around here," she said. "Let's work our way back home by the river, there are a couple of more—"

"What was that?"

"Gunshot," Calico said. "Hush a minute," she said, listening to the sharp sound echo. Two more reports came in rapid succession.

"They've found pa!" Gabe said anxiously, and took off running.

Calico was out of breath and Irish was holding his healed but still-tender ribs, with Jerry bringing up the rear as they straggled over the scree and across the graves. A fire burned in the yard, some distance from the porch, and people were milling about it. Jobeth was giving out inhuman hysterical screams. Through the window, Calico could see Winnie and Ginny hovering, trying to calm her. The boys hung back, their faces reflecting their mother's fear. In the yard, Christian was near the fire, sagging on his crutches. Calico thought the worst; that Judalon had been found, and dead. She made directly for the fire, where Jobediah was adding whole pine logs. God! but Jobeth's caterwauling was unnerving.

"What's happened. Did you find him?" She didn't look behind but sensed Irish and Jerry close. The leaping flames provided welcome warmth. She stripped off her gloves, holding her hands as close to the fire as she dared.

Jebediah arranged yet another log, then straightened up slowly, his bones snapping and groaning with age. "We found a gimme hat, red, held down with a rock, back on the other side of that escarpment." He flung his hand out, indicating the ridge across the river. Calico felt her knees go weak.

"No!" Her insides were screaming with shock.

Jebediah's face was grim.

"It's the same shaft that killed McKenzie," muttered Christian, emitting the words from a pain-filled depth. His face was dull lead gray, and his voice barely audible above Jobeth's continued hysteria. Calico moved around to her grandfather's side. Passing Jerry, she said, "Please, go see if you can get Jobeth calmed."

After a few minutes a deathly silence settled. Phillip appeared, handing out steaming cups of coffee laced with brandy, then he hunkered down next to Irish, engaging him in quiet conversation. Others came outside, milled around, then went back into the cabin. Someone brought Christian a chair and he fell into it. Calico squatted down beside him, staring into the fire. She heard no talk, saw no one, nor did she feel the cold on her back or the warmth of the flames. She was in the shaft, on her hands and knees, then her belly, slithering along, feeling the mountain trembling, talking, warning her...a sacred place.

"I'll have to go in grampa," she said finally. "There's no one else and I know the shaft." She didn't look at him or at Irish, as she slowly became aware of his eyes boring into her.

"You can't go." Christian's voice ebbed with stifled emotions. "I forbid it. The mountain has taken everyone I've ever loved from me. You're all I got left. No." He leaned forward, resting his elbow on his knees, his great shaggy head bent forward, staring at the ground. Calico thought he might be praying. She urged him indoors, but he refused. The wind made the flames slant, golden shards of light that highlighted the strained expressions of the people who huddled around it.

Calico leaned against her grandfather's knee. She was afraid and she shouldn't be. Hadn't she sprung from the bowels of the mountain? And where it glossed over its mud slicks and scars with new growths of mountain laurel, stumpy pines and wild hay, she covered her hurts, her wants and her needs with a mobile mouth that offered arch smiles and silence. And, oh, how she was hurting right this moment. And she had no smile, and her need now could only be fulfilled by the man whose face she glimpsed in the flickering light.

Through a thick fringe of lashes she watched Irish leave Phillip's side, edging his way toward her with that indolent seductive stride of his. It took her by surprise time and time again that she knew his lean muscular body, the shape of his hand and the way they moved on parts of her that she'd never let anyone else touch or see. When he was at her side, she stood up, looked full at him, but didn't speak. There must have been some body language, some lift to the set of her shoulders, the tautness of her jaw, an acceptance in her silvery eyes, because he took her by her arm and propelled her away from the fire into the cold shadows.

"Phillip told me Judalon's in that old mining shaft. I know what you're thinking and you can't do it." There was a kind of thin panic in his voice. Calico shook the sound out of her head. Fear and panic before she ever crawled into the shaft wouldn't do. It would kill her, and Judalon—if she found him still alive.

"I have to, and I'll have to go in tonight. He's already been down there two days...and it may be too late already." She swallowed hard, but there was no saliva, her mouth was so dry. "I—I hate him, but I

have to go for Jobeth and his sons, don't you see?"
She met his gaze with her own and shivered.

While she stood there he unbuttoned her coat, then
his and pulled her into his warmth and their arms
went about each other, and he bent his lips to her ear.
"Listen to me, this is no game you're playing...or I'm
playing...." She tried to close out the desperate
whispers, his breath coming in vapory little puffs, but
it felt so wonderfully good to be in his arms she closed
her eyes, resting her head against his shoulder, her
lips buried in his throat.

There was something dark and growing inside him,
pushing against his chest. His voice cracked. "There's
something...I don't know what it is, but I was never
adoptable. There's something wrong with me. My
soul is dead...was dead, you brought it to life...are
you laughing at me...?"

"No, no, I'm listening." His arms tightened as did
his voice.

"Since I've been on Talking Rock I've often had the
feeling that I was one with the universe...like the
first man. I took up medicine because I wanted to find
out what was wrong with me...and there's nothing—God! I'm as healthy as a horse—"

"You're all mixed up, Irish." Her words were muffled against the thick cords of his neck.

"No! No, I'm not. Quit doing that; your nose is
cold. I was mixed up but I'm not now. I see it, even if
I'm not making it clear. I'm going to stop leaving
notes behind. I don't have a father—at least not one
willing. I accept it. Maybe *I'll* go looking for *him*. It's
what I should have done, but you see, I wanted to be
wanted."

She smiled, a soft slight curve of her mouth. "You're
no different from anyone else."

"Stop making it sound so simple. It isn't." The
words seemed wrung from him, as if they were a ma-

lignant growth he was excising. "I've never had any luck in my entire life, except maybe falling in that damned river...." Suddenly his hands moved to her shoulders, grasping them as if he wanted to shake her. "Calico! Do you understand what I'm saying?"

"Yes," she said slowly. "You're scared for me. You think I might die down in the shaft, and you're telling me all the things that have hurt you, because if I die, it'll be the greatest hurt of all. I think you don't want to lose me."

He stared at her face for an eternity. "You're incredible," he finally whispered, and his lips came down on hers with a brutal harshness, cold at first, then warming as his tongue thrust into her with such savage longing she nearly fainted. The kiss went on and on as if feeding on some forbidden succulence until she was compelled by the hot blood pulsing throughout her to thrust her own tongue into his moist sucking mouth with a savagery that matched his own. She was bereft of oxygen by the time he withdrew and held her pressed against him as if he'd never let her go.

After several seconds she felt impelled to speak. "I don't feel like I'm going to die, and now you've told me all your secrets. When I get mad at you, I'll use them, you know...." She was talking of the future, strongly, with certainty.

"Reminding me of how much of a fool I've been will keep me in line," he answered wryly. "On Monday, I'm filing for divorce in Atlanta. I don't want that standing between us. But it may get nasty...."

"If I told you my secret, you may not want me," she said, testing him, testing herself, to see if she could come close to mouthing the words, putting them into shape, forming the sounds, telling the event that had held her to the mountain, encompassing her in loneliness.

"I'll always want you. There's nothing that could keep me from wanting you...."

She wanted to believe him desperately, but the courage to say more lodged beyond her reach, so she moved on to the pressing present. "Stay by grampa while I'm down, will you? Keep him company. Waiting is the worst part. But I'll be all right, I promise."

He was nibbling at her earlobe, his breath so nice and warm. "Suppose you get hung up or stuck...?"

She gave a small laugh. "If Judalon got through as big as he is, I will, too."

"Let me go with you. I'll follow you in."

She thought about the darkness, the closeness, the tons of mountain surrounding the tunnel and how in panic, a scream could bring it all crushing down; she thought about how men far stronger and braver than herself had, in the dim wet interior of a shaft, suddenly suffered claustrophobia and in the fear, their hurry to the surface, had been lost, injured or killed. "No—" She started to say it was too dangerous, catching it back just in time. "I'll feel safe with you feeding the lifeline, the rope."

"I don't know if I can let you go. What's it like?" He left off nibbling her ear, but held her tightly, so that the long length of him was imprinted on her.

"Cold, but not as cold as it is up here right now, and wet, but from the feel of this air, you're going to be wetter. It's dark and really close in some places, only inches to spare." In her mind she was already mapping her path, wondering how far in Judalon had gotten, wondering which tunnel he had taken, man-made or natural, and if she could tell. She turned her head, looking toward the escarpment, seeing the shape of it in her mind, for now, in the dark, it was distorted. Of all the mines on the mountain, she mused, why did Judalon have to choose the one that was her father's grave? Hackles cut a path down her spine and she was seized by icy fingers. "We'd better go in now," she said in a quavering voice. "There's Jeb on the porch, looking for us, I think."

16

CALICO EXPECTED THE WARMTH OF THE CABIN to embrace her. But it didn't. She carried the cold in with her, the icy fingers seemed to spread. There was an air of expectancy circulating, and all eyes lifted and locked on her as she entered ahead of Irish.

Someone had finally convinced her grandfather to move indoors and he was sitting at the table, sorting equipment she would need. Beside his chair lay a coil of rope. Winnie pressed coffee into her hands. Calico accepted it absently. "Where's Jobeth?" she asked.

"In your room lying down."

The boys were sitting on the sofa, or the floor at the hearth, being entertained by Jerry Bass. Phillip and Ginny were at the table, interested spectators. For several silent heartbeats she resented everyone in the cabin, every living human on the mountain, the interruption of her well-ordered life and then the feeling passed and there was no more time for thoughts. There was only the preparation of equipment to take into the mine, and of herself. She set her coffee aside and began to inspect the rope.

"It's frayed in some places," she said to her grandfather, "and I'll need at least another 250 more feet. I don't want to go in with less than 500."

Gabe was dispatched to the work shed with lantern to find more coils while Christian silently ran the rope through his fingers, stopping at places Calico indicated to cut and resplice it.

"You want to take any food?" Winnie asked. Birdlike, she had been fluttering around, trying to hide her nervousness and not managing at all.

"No food. Just water, flashlights, my knife—"

"A harness?" injected Jebediah.

"No. I've only been in up to 100 or so feet and it was close then...I wouldn't have any maneuverability." The harness was discarded.

"Hard hat?"

"No. But extra batteries if we have them, and matches. Kitchen matches and a piece of candle."

"Calico!"

It was Jobeth, still distraught, but obviously slightly drunk, so that Calico knew what had been used to finally calm her. Her dimensions seemed vast in her pregnancy, and the manner in which she lurched to the table would have been comical under other circumstances. She clung to the back of the nearest chair, her gaze riveted on Calico.

"I know about you." she rasped out, tongue loosened by whiskey. "I know what Judalon done. Your name came up between us this summer—"

Calico came out of her chair so fast, it flew out behind her, landing with a crash. Wildly, like a caged animal, she glanced at the faces around the table, feeling all hollow inside, as if she couldn't breathe, as if there was no room for any more air. "Shut up! Jobeth. Shut up!" Racing around the table, she grabbed Jobeth's arm, trying to drag her back into the bedroom, but Jobeth shook her off.

"Leave me alone. I just want to know...if...." She nearly choked and her words began to slur. "When you find Judalon, and he ain't dead, are you going to bring him out."

Calico went white about her lips and didn't dare look toward Irish. Oh, what must he be thinking? "Yes, Jobeth, of course I'm going to bring him out." *If I can.*

"I wouldn't blame you none; I wouldn't," sniffed Jobeth. "He always praised you over me...but I—I love him." She began to wail then, and Calico with Winnie urged her to bed again, but Jobeth kept on.

"Leave us," Calico ordered to Winnie. "And close the door." When she heard the door slam, she shook Jobeth's shoulders. "Now listen to me, Jobeth. You must never, ever speak of this—ever! Do you hear me?"

"He loves you more 'n he does me."

"No! What happened, happened a long time ago, before you got married, and Judalon was drunk," she added, inspired to lie. "You can't fault a man for doing something when he's drunk, can you? And there's never been another time. Judalon's never come near me since."

"Fact?" Jobeth questioned.

"Fact, Jobeth. I swear."

"On your mother's grave?"

"On my mother's grave."

"Have I blasphemed?" Jobeth wanted to know. "Have I?" She moved her hand protectively over her protruding stomach. "Have I sinned, taking God's number for my own? Am I being punished?"

"No. There's just been an accident. Judalon just wanted to provide for you, give you a better life, that's why he went treasure hunting." She nearly gagged on the words. The hate she felt for Judalon welled up inside her, a living thing, and afraid that Jobeth would see it, turned her face away and found herself staring into the frozen, glittering green eyes of Irish.

She couldn't muster up enough air in her lungs even to gasp. "How long—?" she choked. "How long have you been standing there?" her eyes clung to him, but she couldn't see what was going on behind them. His face seemed gray as if all his blood had drained out, giving him the look of some granite-carved god.

"What did Tarrant do to you?" His voice was lined with something she couldn't name. Pain? If not, she knew not what. She rose to her feet draggingly, seeming to weigh a thousand pounds.

"We—we were discussing something that happened years ago. It doesn't concern you." She felt like pieces of her were falling away.

"How many years?" he asked, stiff lipped. "What was yesterday morning all about?"

"Yesterday? Yesterday? What happened yesterday?" Jobeth asked, alarmed, the suspicion in her tone as open as Irish's.

"Nothing. I saw Judalon for a minute, asked him how you were, that's all. He didn't act like he wanted to talk to me. I guess it was because he was looking for gold on my mountain." Looking at Irish, Calico dared him to dispute this. "I have to go now," she said. "Every hour counts against Judalon."

"Tell him I—I ain't mad with him no more," Jobeth said haltingly.

"I'll tell him." Calico replied, and pushing past Irish, she left the room.

Feeling transparent as she stood at the stove warming her hands with her back to the room, Calico thought, *let them stare*. She knew everyone's eyes were on her because the room was permeated with that strange awkward silence that follows a social blunder.

The warmth from the stove was coming in waves and closing her eyes, she could feel it against her eyelids like a caress. She would love a bath. Thinking of Judalon, seeing him or even talking of him always made her want to be fresh, clean. Her life was divided: *Before* Judalon—*after* Judalon, like diet ads in magazines. Before...she had been aware of her body, its emerging shapes, each softening curve, the graceful line of her legs, her flat taut belly, and afterward . . . she had wanted to scrape the skin from her bones.

She had discovered nothing showed on the outside. It seemed impossible, but it didn't. So she took care of herself meticulously, guarding her secret as she guarded her hoard of gold. Her softness, her cleanliness had just been a clever deception to hide her shame. And the funny part was, what she fought against with Judalon, she craved from Irish McCaulley. It didn't make sense.

"We ought to get started," Jebediah said, touching her arm, breaking her reverie. As she slipped into her jacket, she accepted a chorus of good-lucks solemnly given by the boys and Ginny.

Phillip, Jerry and Irish were going across the river and up the escarpment with them. When Christian rose lumberingly from his chair, she protested. "No, grampa, you stay here."

"I won't and that's that," he muttered, and signaled Gabe and Frank to stay at his side. The boys leaped to do his bidding, relieved with the chance to be included.

It couldn't be said that anyone was happy, yet there was a sense of excitement for the out of ordinary as they gathered on the front porch and began to shoulder equipment. Winnie moved among them wringing her hands, repeating monotonously, like a chant, "It ain't fittin', it ain't fittin' for Calico to be the one." Jebediah ushered her inside the cabin, cooing gently in his old man's voice.

Calico was caught in the excitement too, but there was something she had to do first. She picked up one of the portable lanterns, stepped off the porch and strode purposefully up to the scree. She was feeling the need to touch consecrated ground, to ask the protection of her mother's spirit. In passing she touched the leaning cross above her father's hollow grave, and shivered. Did his soul roam the sacred tunnel?

She sat on the stump, the lamp between her feet, watching leaves pushed by the wind tumble into the lamp glow, then disappear into the night. She felt an affinity with the leaves. Spawned by a sturdy tree, they unfurled their new green shoots, blossoming, and were allowed to live but a single season. Her whole life, up to now, had been but a single season.

An eerie cord of lightning shot from the sky, illuminating the surrounding hummock, and that instant was all she needed to see Irish standing at the edge of her mother's grave, a heavy coil of rope looped over his shoulder.

"I think there's one thing I don't like about you," she said, "This sneaking up on people." She was still miserably vexed at finding him eavesdropping on her conversation with Jobeth.

He made no move to come nearer. "What you're doing is quixotic," he said disapprovingly.

"Not quixotic—necessary—and I know the mine."

He stepped forward then and tossed a pair of hip boots at her feet. "Jeb says to tell you to put these on, for fording the river." Silently, but aware that he was watching her, she tugged on the rubbers over her leather boots. The air was electric with his unspoken thoughts. Still she wasn't prepared for his attack.

"You lied to Jobeth." His voice was wire taut, nearly devoid of inflection, but the accusation hung bitterly between them.

Calico moved like a somnambulist, picking up the blanket roll, the lantern, stepping past Irish, forcing her brain to single out an answer. "I said what I did to calm her. She's overwrought, scared and drunk."

"Scared and a little bit tipsy, yes, but she spoke the truth. Have you been using me to make Tarrant jealous? Are you lovers?"

She spun about, the lantern flying in a wide arc, thinking she was screaming, yet she spoke only in a hoarse whisper. "Is that what you think?"

"Never mind what I think," he said grimly. "I've been through one marriage with a woman who spent her spare time bed hopping. I'm not making that mistake again."

"So, don't!" she spat, feeling all used up and bruised, hurting because he didn't trust her and not able to make it right without admitting her shame.

17

"WANT TO TALK ABOUT IT?" Jerry Bass asked, sidling up to her.

Calico dismissed him with a curt no.

"Do you think it's a good idea to attempt any sort of rescue in the mood you're in?" he coaxed.

"I don't need a psychiatrist."

Unabashed, Jerry pressed, "I'm talking to you as a friend. I saw and so did everyone else, the look on your face and that of McCaulley when you walked into camp. Is it just a lovers' quarrel, or more serious?"

Calico hesitated, taking care not to glance at Irish who stood some distance away. They had not spoken for the past thirty minutes. She yearned to retract every suspicious, angry word that had flared between them and begin again. But you couldn't undo words like you could a knot in string. "You're a man," she said finally. "What can you know about how a woman feels?"

"A lot," Jerry answered, but knowing it was no use, moved away.

EVERYONE WATCHED Calico expectantly, for she was ready to enter the mine. Behind her, in the lee of a granite boulder a fire blazed; in front of her the slit in the face of the mountain glared back at her like the dark empty socket of a one-eyed cyclops. At her feet was the red cap belonging to Judalon, turned up and filled with gravel. A grave marker, mountain folks called it. She tried to push the thought from her mind.

Calico moved toward the opening, Jebediah following, his squat broad shoulders draped with twin spirals of rope, the end of which was woven about her belt at her side, an umbilical cord to mark her passage into the womb of the mountain.

There was a sudden commotion several yards down the mountain. Calico turned, making out the unmistakable silhouette of a quilt-clad Jobeth, leaning heavily on Ginny. *No!* Calico thought. She couldn't bear another confrontation.

Almost as one the men turned to face the approaching women. Calico caught her grandfather's eye as he was tossing away his crutches to sit near the mouth of the mine. "Feed me the rope," she said in a quiet voice. "I'm going in." She turned on the flashlight, aiming its powerful beam into the shaft, moving it slowly, peering into each crevice, each cool shadow that might hold living danger, and in the next instant she slipped into the mine. Its dank, screaming silence engulfed her.

"SHE INSISTED," Ginny was saying of Jobeth, as they neared the log fire. "Winnie's watching the children. I felt I had to come with her."

Jobeth was breathing hard, gasping for air, holding her great stomach as she looked into the shadows. "I've got to talk to Calico. I've got to!"

"Too late now," Christian said. "She's gone." And he leaned back against the boulder, his gaze falling to his lap as the rope threaded between his thick old fingers, snaking its way with thin rustlings onto the floor of the mountain and disappearing into its depth.

Irish heard the old man's words disbelievingly, and as the fact of them shot into his brain he stood rooted to the ground, unable to move, as if he'd just been struck by lightning.

"Help these women back to the cabin, Gabe," Jebediah ordered. "Your mother's in no condition to be facing this weather. And this is a man's work here."

"Wait...wait!" Jobeth pleaded, hearing the forbidding tone and knowing she had been turned back. She cast about the shadows until she spotted Irish. "I've got to say something to Professor McCaulley."

Dazed, Irish stepped forward. "What's that, Mrs. Tarrant?"

"I said private!" Jobeth screamed, as everyone began to cluster around. They backed away at once in the face of her hysteria.

"I—I shouldn'ta said what I did," she blurted to Irish. "When you was in the room. I knew you were there, and knowed all along that Calico didn't."

He was trying to remember a prayer, any prayer, something that would get God's attention to keep Calico safe. With great difficulty he focused on Jobeth. "What are you trying to tell me, Mrs. Tarrant?"

"That—that Calico ain't never liked Judalon—ever. Long about the end of this summer he got drunk, we had a fight, and well...he throwed her name up to me...she's always been prettier than me...it ain't her fault...but she never married, but that ain't here nor there," Jobeth said, beginning to run her sentences together, hurrying to get shed of the guilt she was feeling. "After the fight, I got to thinking...Calico ain't never come around our place when Judalon was to home...never asked about him.... Funny, I hadn't noticed, but we were always took up with the kids and such." Jobeth hung her head and began to sob. "Judalon took her...."

Irish felt this incredible pain behind his breastbone. "What do you mean, took her?"

Jobeth glanced at his face and took a step back. "Took her, forced her...." She swallowed. "Brought shame on her." The wind was whipping her hair, making her look like a wild woman, but it was nothing compared to the horrified expression growing on Irish's face as the realization of what Jobeth was saying dawned on him. She reached out to touch Irish, bring him back to reality. "I've been harboring hard feelings all these months, trying to fault Calico with it since I found out. It ain't something a woman wants to know about her man. I just wanted to tell her, before she...I know she's going after Judalon for me, I never doubted it. It's just...if Calico finds Judalon dead, she's liable to just sit right down inside that mountain and let herself die, too. She's strong-minded thataway, once she makes up her mind...."

The sound that escaped Irish's throat was nothing human.

He began running toward the mouth of the mine.

"Whoa!" Jebediah bellowed. "What in tarnation! Stop him!" Phillip dove for Irish and missed; as Irish tried to sidestep Christian, Jerry Bass loomed out of the shadowed dark.

"Dr. McCaulley, I admire you, and I'm awfully sorry to have to do this," and his right hand came up in a fist and connected solidly with Irish's stubborn jaw. Phillip, running up and breathless, caught him as he collapsed.

"Throw a blanket over him and lay him out over here by me," Christian said. Then, to Jerry, "I reckon you ought not be in his line of vision when he wakes."

"I couldn't agree with you more," Jerry said sheepishly, nursing his fist, which he was certain was broken into a thousand little fragments. Picking up a blanket roll, he stepped away from the firelight, and made himself comfortable beneath the charred remains of a tree that had long lost a battle with a bolt of lightning.

Gabe and Ginny ushered a moaning Jobeth down

the mountain, and soon the only sounds were those of the damp wind soughing, pine knots bursting in the fire and the rope as it slithered between Christian's fingers. And then all thoughts turned toward the fathomless subterranean abyss and Calico—except those of Christian. He was staring at the unconscious form of Irish McCaulley, thinking, he's just like his pa, always butting in and joining a scrap.

CALICO STARED WITH INCREDULITY at the wall of crushed rock and rubble that blocked her path. On her hands and knees, for there was little headspace, she swung a beam of light over the pile, covering every inch, looking for a hole. Judalon had come this way, she had found signs...boot scrapings in the damp, gritrock-strewn tunnel, places on rough dark walls where he had hammered and nicked at...with his pick looking for gold.

Moving closer and crouching carefully so that she wouldn't dislodge the tons of rubble, she examined it more fully, trying to determine if it was a new fall or old, but the entire mountain, inside and out, was ancient, thousands and thousands of years, thrown up in an upheaval and heated beyond measure. Her inspection told her nothing and raised new questions. Was Judalon held fast and forever beneath the rock in front of her, had he gone beyond it before it collapsed, had he backed out, forgetting to pick up his marker, or was there another passage and she'd missed it?

Sighing, she wriggled backward until she had room to half sit, half lounge, listening all the while for the creaking, the murmuring of the spirits, but hearing nothing outside her own labored breathing. Her mouth was dry, caked with dust millenniums old. She stood the flashlight on its end, illuminating the low ceiling as she hauled her flat canteen from her backpack and slaked her thirst. As she tipped her head back she saw the narrow slit, like the wide grinning mouth of a monster. Cautiously she reached up and ran her fingers about its rim, then she struck a match, watching the flame hold steady, then flicker, nudged by a dank and sour air.

Her heart began to pound erratically as she inspected this new tunnel. A natural excavation, it had a depth of only eighteen inches narrowing at each side, and it ascended. It meant going in on her belly, using her elbows to pull herself forward. She adjusted her equipment to lie alongside her, the backpack, her canteen, checking that her knife was firmly in its scabbard, and that's when she discovered she'd run out of lifeline. She considered her predicament for only a moment, then in a swirl of frenzy, hurrying so that she wouldn't change her mind, she scrabbled back to saw off twenty feet of the thin sisal to take with her.

Every yard gained assaulted her senses, becoming sheer torture. She rolled and slithered over jagged rocks, cutting her elbows, scraping buttons off her flannel shirt, ripping her thermal undershirt down to flesh that was soon bruised and raw. She had to shove with her feet, lay the flashlight aside, pulling forward with her hands to make any headway, twisting and turning, contorting her body like an acrobat at practice to move around sharp curves, to slither up or unexpectedly slide downward. It was as if having entered the grinning mouth of the monster, it was determined to swallow her, suffocate her, gulping her down its gullet into its bowels.

There was an ominous rumbling, gently at first, like the soft gurgling at the back of a throat. She only heard it, feeling no vibrations. If the mountain came crashing, crushing down upon her, she'd never know. But there was no way to look behind or see around the corner in front, so she kept very still, trying not to think, not to feel, struggling to contain a spreading fear, the claustrophobia that every miner dreads. Her skin felt prickly, her brow and armpits filled with sweat.

She switched off the flashlight, laying her head on her open palm, taking deep breaths, recalling what old-timers had told her to do...breathe evenly... *evenly*, she screamed at herself, hearing the rasping of her lungs. Close your eyes, visualize something... anything...not the walls closing in, above all, don't move, not yet...not yet...a move in panic meant certain death. She thought of Irish, the shape of his hands, counting in her mind's eye every tiny wiry tuft of hair on his knuckles, saw his hands moving over her tawny skin; met his eyes, green and heavily lidded, filled with an urgency she could put to rest; she moistened her lips with her tongue, imagining Irish's there, warm and strangely rough, thrusting into pink softness and oh, he was so naked, so hard, teaching her the mysteries of love, and she realized with a start that these thoughts were doing nothing to curb her rapid breathing, so she forced them away and focused on the serenity of a sunrise; all red and gold with birds chirping, her chickens beginning to stir and cluck, the soft sounds of the river splashing placidly...drifting...drifting with the river, until she opened her eyes to the pitch blackness and there *was* a steady drip, drip, drip of water coming from somewhere.

She cocked her head to listen. After a moment she switched on the light and began to inch forward, stopping now and again to listen for the water. The shaft became narrower, and she had to remove her backpack, shoving it, along with the coil of rope and water canteen in front of her. Shove, slither, shove, slither, until she shoved once and suddenly the pack disappeared and she heard a thunk.

"Who's there? Who's there?" A voice, thin and echoing weakly, moved past her. She moved forward, hurrying, and almost slipped into the chasm, catching herself only just in time. When her heart stopped thundering, she answered.

"It's me. Calico."

She heard a low wail. "I shoulda knowed they'd send you...I shoulda knowed. Oh, I'm a dead man, sure," Judalon kept saying over and over like a litany.

"Stop your whining," she hissed, aware of her own edge of fear, and not yet able to deal with his. "Where are you?" She aimed the light, searching upward, seeing a cambered roof, curving in the middle, some sort of cave or cavern or well, and she was on a shelf several yards below its ceiling. A riffle of water beads sped through the light beam.

"Down here," Judalon groaned, and Calico flashed the light into the well below, seeing nothing, the shaft seemingly too deep for the light to carry.

"Can you see the light?" she called.

"Yes...."

"I'm going to aim it on the wall, you tell me where you're at from it."

A long pause. "Yeah," he said, resignedly "You're forty feet above me and to my left...twenty feet... more left...ten feet...you passed over my head." Finally she found him, a gray shape huddled against a boulder.

"How'd you get down there?"

"Fell. There's a ridge, spiraling down. I was following it. It gave way. You ain't never goin' to git me out. I'm hurt, too. You better back out, save yourself."

"That's mighty generous of you, Judalon, after all you've done...."

"I never meant you no harm, Calico," he wheedled, his voice sounding eerie, coming as it did from the dark depths of the pit. She resented him speaking of those things now. They both knew what he meant. For years she had hated, and hated good, wishing a vengeance upon him. He had taken from her the right to hope, her dreams, her girlhood, the privilege to offer herself in marriage without guilt or shame. And now... now, she thought wearily, rubbing a palm across her face, she had to save him somehow, send him back into the bosom of his family and Jobeth.

"You still there?" he called, sounding fearful that she might not be.

"Yes. Be quiet a minute, Judalon. Let me think. How far do you think you fell?"

"Fifteen feet, maybe more, and it's wet down here."

Calico sucked in her breath. "How wet?"

"Water's risen two inches since I been here. I figure when it rains and the river rises, this hole catches overflow from the river somewhere... it's why the walls are so slick, and some of the rocks are covered with acorn barnacles."

"Can you see where my pack fell?" she asked, leaning over the lip of the shaft, shining her light straight down.

Can't see nothing but your light, and couldn't get to it iff'n I did; something's terrible wrong with my legs."

She wished now that she had brought the harness. Getting down presented only a small problem. Coming up again was the real hurdle, especially if she had to haul Judalon.... The thought trailed off. She couldn't admit defeat—not yet.

It took her an hour to reach him, hugging the spiral shelf, descending inch by painful inch, but able to step across the section that had disintegrated with Judalon's weight. Weary beyond measure, she sank down into the slush beside him, swinging the beam of light.

"What's wrong with your legs?"

"Don't know exactly. Can't feel them. I've got an

ache low in my back though." He was trying to be brave and failed miserablly. "We're gonna die...."

She swung the light away from him, embarrassed to watch him cry, despising him for what he had done to her, for what he was demanding of her now. Comfort. She found her knapsack, the rope, pulled out the candle and lit it, scrounging for a rock to set it on.

"Gawd! That looks good," Judalon exclaimed, when it flared up, casting a two-foot circle. She gave him her canteen and he drank greedily. "Did you bring any food? I'm hungry."

"You should have gone home and had the Thanksgiving dinner Jobeth cooked for you," she said, taking perverse pleasure in his discomfort, then going silent when she recognized an irritating twitch of pricked conscience. For once in his life, Judalon had the sense to hold his tongue.

Calico sloshed around in the mud, looking for a dry shelf, remembering the dark menacing clouds threatening rain...rain to fill up the river making it slide over its banks, and somehow fill up this well in the deep labyrinth of the mountain. There was none, so she gathered rocks and small boulders, piling them up to create a perch of sorts. It wasn't a feather bed exactly, but at least they'd be out of the water—for a while.

"It's no sense trying to make things better," Judalon said, following her slender shadowy figure with his eyes. "Not for me anyway. I ain't going to walk out of here."

Perhaps neither of them would, Calico thought.

It was a struggle to move him. "Oh, Lord!" he shrieked when she grabbed him beneath his arms and pulled him onto the rubble. She forced herself to sit next to him, hating it that her shoulder should rub his.

"What happens when the candle burns out," he asked.

"We'll use the flashlight and when that goes, we'll just be in the dark. But I'll figure something out before then. Now, try and get some sleep. I need to rest a few minutes myself."

"I can't sleep. I've been trying for two days. All that happens when I close my eyes is, I keep seeing everything I ever done... that's how I know I'm going to die. They say when you do, your whole life flashes before you...."

"Judalon," said Calico with a tenacity that clung to her words, "after I rest, and get some strength back, I'm going to haul you up that wall if I have to drag you feet first. Now, shut up."

"I want to tell you I'm sorry for what I done to you," he said.

It was a squalid plea, one hard for her to accept. "Sorry! Sorry!" she erupted. "You ruined my life, and you've kept on ruining it. If you think I'm going to sit here next to you and listen to your... your confession so you can wipe the slate clean, you're wrong. Dead wrong." Her hand traveled to the knife at her waist and in the dim light, Judalon did not miss the slight movement.

"Let me explain," he told her, his voice rising. "Jobeth egged me, kept talking about how I was a real he-man... and we were going to get married. I hadn't ever had a woman and she would of knowed... she would of—"

Raw bile rose up in Calico's throat. "You mean... you mean I was just *practice*?"

"You don't know how it is with a man, Calico," he whined. "It ain't like a woman. And Jobeth, she wanted seven children, trying to make herself a saint doin' God's work before she's even dead. That scares a man, and that's all she ever wanted me for." He began

to cry, great heaving wrenching sobs that unnerved
Calico. "I ain't goin' to be no use to her no more. I can
tell. I can't feel a thing. My back's broken, sure."

Calico digested what Judalon had said. The bitter
feelings she harbored against him had not prepared
her for this, that he was so transparent in his wish to
be liked, to be a man...and she wondered how he
could have done the things he did, stealing, fighting,
drinking, and other things...and still expect people to
admire him. The hate she was feeling for him slid a
little off-center, and pity edged with disgust filled the
space. Winnie was right, she thought. Pride could
hurt and destroy, pride could mangle people as much
as it could do good. There was an odd convergence of
all her emotions; of pain, of love, of hate, of confusion, and she knew she had held herself in bondage,
enduring, but not accepting. "Go to sleep, Judalon,"
she suggested in a tone far more kindly than she
would ever have believed it possible to speak to him.

"Then you forgive me?" he choked.

I can't! I can't! She had an inkling now that some
men, and women, no matter how long they lived,
never sipped that sweet nectar called love, never suc-
cumbed to that feeling that made you all trembly inside, but she had—with Irish. And somewhere deep
inside her there was an intimate severance with her
past. A lovely autumn day when there had been an
act of defilement. "It's in the past, best forgotten," she
said.

She pulled her shirt about her, locking her arms
around her knees, resting her head upon them, willing sleep to come.

18

SHE WAS ADRIFT with the spirits. It was cold and dark. She was in her father's grave and he was calling to her, clamoring for attention, his voice filling the cavern with a cadence that ricocheted off the walls of her soul. Then the voice became louder, desperate, warning her, and she came awake with a jolt and the voice was still calling.

"Calico! Calico! Answer me, damn you!"

God in heaven! "Irish! Is that you? But how..." she called, stumbling to her feet in the dark.

"Up here. They tried to stop me," he said. His jaw still felt as though it were wrapped around the back of his neck, but that had become the least of his worries once he had crawled into the shaft. There would be time to talk of that later. Now, he just wanted to get Calico out. She moved into the beam of light he played around into the hole.

"I can't believe it's really you," she said, the tone of her voice echoing the truth of her statement. "Weren't you scared?"

"For you. It kept me going." The truth was that he had been fighting claustrophobia from the moment he had slipped into the cavelike tunnel. He had felt the walls closing in on him, heard his heart thumping in his chest, heard every single intake of breath. Telling himself to turn back hundreds of times, he had driven himself forward only because he thought Calico might be around the next curve, that she might be hurt, that she might be lost to him forever if he didn't keep going. But he didn't know how to tell her these things, not yet. "How'd you get down there? Are you all right?"

"I'm fine. I went around the edge of a narrow ledge, but you'd better not try it."

"Did you find Tarrant?" he asked.

"Yes. He's down here, asleep."

"Well, wake him up and let's get the hell out of here," Irish told her in no uncertain terms.

"Judalon's hurt; he can't walk," and she explained to him their predicament.

"I don't know what made me do it," Irish said, after listening to her, "but I rolled up a hundred feet of the rope where you'd cut it and brought it with me. Tie Tarrant's feet together, and then wrap the rest around him like you were winding thread on a spool. That's about the most bracing we can give him. Can you get back up here where I am?"

"Yes." She would, she could, if she had to climb the vertical slimy walls with her bare hands.

"Hauling him up like that might—"

Irish seemed to be reading her mind. "He hasn't a chance any other way."

After that they only talked to one another in clipped tones, a word of direction here, an order to stop there while every ounce of energy remaining to them was used to move Judalon up the wall to the lip of the tunnel, inch by painful inch. Calico worked at Irish's side, their bodies prone, touching, both breathing hard, panting, tiring, stopping, beginning again against the weight of Judalon, whose screams echoed chillingly until he fainted, and then his weight seemed to increase by a thousand pounds. Finally he was on the ledge with them, and for the next few hours Calico had the sense of being in a film. As they pushed and shoved and groaned and contorted their bodies and Judalon's to make their way to safety, her emotions

seemed to curl back on themselves like the backwash
of a wave rolling out to the sea. And all the while she
wondered how she could put into words what Judalon had done to her, wondered how she could tell
Irish of that horrible day that she had hoped would lie
in the back of her mind until she died...and wondered mostly if he would still have her.

IT WAS JUST COMING DAWN when they came out of the
shaft, weary beyond belief, haggard, caked with mud
and dust. The cold air was sweet after the musky
vapid dampness of the mountain's heart. The menacing heavy clouds had swept northeast, carrying their
rain with them, leaving the mountain flush with the
sun's hidden rays.

Word of the rescue had traveled like forest fire out
of control and the mountainside was crowded with
neighbors and strangers. Blankets were thrown about
Calico's and Irish's shoulders. They were led to an old
log that had been rolled up to the fire, mugs of steaming coffee thrust into their hands. A sense of urgency
was all around them, with bits and snatches of conversations coming to them like some far-off signal.
The sheriff was there, a reporter, a photographer.

Judalon was transported to the hospital, where Doc
Willis had taken Jobeth during the night to have her
baby. The Sheriff took Calico's and Irish's statements,
given haltingly between great gulps of air, and refills
of coffee. The reporter listened and the photographer
snapped picture after picture until Calico pulled the
blanket over her head.

And then everything sounded remote, unreal.

Winnie stomped up to where Calico was sitting
hunched beneath the blanket and scoured the girl
with her gaze from head to toe, seeing for herself that
Calico was alive. "I asked the Lord to spare you and
he did," she said, and looking over at Irish, added,

"Him, too," as if Irish was an interloper deserving only of a footnote to her prayers. Then with a clucking and hissing she gathered up the remainder of Jobeth's children and took them down the mountain, her mind replete with tale and gossip that would last her through a month of Thursday quilting circles.

Jerry Bass approached and spoke a few low words with Irish, and after shaking his hand, turned to Calico. "I wish I could stay, but I'm sure Dr. Marcavitch is wondering about his wife's car by now." He bent low and whispered in her ear, " If Winnie cooks the wedding supper, invite me," and he was gone before she could form a retort. Wedding supper. Whose wedding?

Phillip, his eyes red-rimmed from lack of sleep, sidled up, accompanied by Willie Boles. "I'm taking Ginny and Sarah back to Atlanta now that all's well," he said, aiming his words at Irish. Willie spat a stream of tobacco juice into the fire, watching it hiss.

"All the crew done showed up for work," he said awkwardly. "Reckon you want us to get started?"

"Thanks, Cups. That'd be fine," Irish told him.

Calico cut a glance at Irish over the rim of her cup. His brilliant green eyes were dulled and sunk far back into his head, his craggy face lined with exhaustion, but she was proud of him. A city man, doing what he had done, crawling into that shaft to find her, and yet, no word of passion or love had passed between them. She felt a dreadful huge lump beginning to form in her throat.

Birds chirped and fluttered in the breaking of the sun over an eastern crest, and suddenly all the activity that had been swirling around them lessened. The crowd—the neighbors, the sheriff with the reporter and photographer trailing behind—moved off down the mountain. There was only Jebediah doing what always had to be done...reclaiming equipment, coiling ropes, gathering lamps and the inumerable bits and pieces that get scattered and left lying around, and her grampa, who came hobbling up to sit near them on a boulder that faced the fire.

"A bath and sleep is what I want," Calico announced in a small tired voice, but somehow not having the strength to move her legs, or detach herself from the log and the blazing warmth of the fire that sent up a trail of smoke to mingle with the gold and purple hues of the sunrise. She watched her grampa settle himself on the boulder and discovered him eyeing Irish with a peculiar expression on his face.

He made a small movement with his gnarled old hands, a seemingly helpless gesture. Irish didn't see it, nor did he see Christian; his mind was elsewhere, his eyes closed, but they flew open at Christian's first words.

For the old man felt the time was upon him, felt it urgently, that the telling of it would somehow expiate his sense of guilt. A guilt that hung heavily about him now that Irish McCaulley had brought Calico out of that killer mountain alive and unhurt. "Your ma was sweet Rosie McCaulley," he said beginning gruffly.

Irish was electrified. "Sweet Rosie McCaulley," he repeated gutturally. Then, "Rose, her name was Rose."

"Your pa never called her anything but sweet Rosie," Christian said, and began to pack his pipe with thick trembling fingers.

"Is this some sort of joke?" Irish asked, unable to keep anger from slipping into his voice. He flashed a look at Calico. "Is nothing sacred in these mountains? What I told you was private."

Calico reeled as though struck. "I haven't said anything, not a single word." She turned to Christian. "Grampa, do you know what you're saying?" she demanded.

Raising his head, Christian looked into Irish's strange green eyes and nodded. "It's my mission."

"Your mission...your mission—I'm so tired of hearing...!" Irish put out his hand, touching her, and she fell silent.

"Wait, let's hear what he has to say." He didn't believe it possible that this old man, light years away from his own life-style, could be telling him about his father. He didn't believe in fate, and with his scientific mind, coincidences could always be explained away. "How? How do you know what my father called my mother?"

"I shared a cell with him for eight years. He told me."

All those years of waiting, of wanting. Blood left Irish's face, sinking somewhere around his ankles, his breathing became shallow so that he could barely articulate. "Cell? Do you mean prison?" No wonder that he felt the urge always to look inside himself, no wonder that his soul seemed so flat and dead. His worst fears were realized. He was the issue of a violent man, he was the residue of life's flotsam. He looked at Calico, at Christian, the thousand questions in his mind reflected in his eyes. On a separate plane he was hearing Sister Antonio's harsh words that he couldn't be adopted. And the irony of it all. Here was an old man, far removed from his past, saying as calmly as you please, "Your ma was sweet Rosie McCaulley. Your pa always called her that." Irish believed him.

"I knew you were Drew's son the minute I laid eyes on you," the old man was saying. "It's what gave me such a shock, I reckon. I thought you were Drew, coming to haunt me. Stranger things have happened on this mountain."

"Drew? Drew who?" Irish moved his head slowly, taking in the fiery ball of sun as it rose higher and higher, illuminating tall stately pines, and the birds taking to wing and he felt as if he were floating with them, climbing, soaring.

"Drew Parsons. Your pa." Christian's eyes went blank as he looked into his past. "And I let him die..." he muttered low, saying the words aloud for the first time in more than thirty years. Saying the words to get shed of them, to finish with the death and guilt that had plagued him this long while.

Irish's lips worked but no sound came forth. Seeing this, Calico thought of all those fluttering notes, those messages left with secretaries or doormen or tacked to locked doors. "How can you know about Irish, grampa? How?" She viewed Irish with a kind of weary fascination, and knew that she loved him beyond anything she'd ever known in her life. It was hurting her to see the hope in his face.

"Prison does strange things to a man," her grampa was murmuring. Irish's attention was riveted on him, and Calico knew that there was no way she could stop her grandfather from talking, from what bore down on him.

"I'd already been there twelve years when Drew came. He was well...different. He was from up north to begin with, and he had strange notions. He shared everything, anything he had, with other inmates. Whatever he had, you had, but he thought everyone else was like that—generous. Men in prison aren't like that. They hoard. Drew shared, but if he wanted a smoke, he took it, or if he needed soap or toothpaste, why, he borrowed that too. I—had a fondness for a special tobacco. Jeb ordered it for me. One afternoon I went back to our cell to find that Drew had smoked the last of it. I never said anything, but it stuck in my craw. Small things take on significances all out of proportion when you're in a cage....

"A week later there was a scuffle in the cell block between a new inmate and a lifer. Drew stepped between them and got stabbed for his trouble with a knife honed from a spoon. He bled to death. I could've saved him, and didn't. I was still mad that he'd used up my tobacco. Can't get it out of my head...never have been able to, till now. I'd taken an oath to save lives. That's the main reason why I never tried to get my license reinstated."

The old man was purging himself. Irish understood that. He understood that he himself had been the catalyst. He saw the pain in the gray-bearded face, but he was so close, too close to his dream not to ask questions. "How do know for sure this Drew Parsons was my father?"

"Men in prison live in the past—their future, well...there isn't any future. So we talked among ourselves. I knew Rosie as well as I knew my own Lucy. She had a son, like I had McKenzie, and Rosie died, like my Lucy died. Rosie's death shattered Drew. He was only nineteen at the time he met her, but his parents wouldn't hear of him marrying her. A maid, especially an Irish Catholic, so he took money from his father's bank and made arrangements for the baby's care with some nuns. Gave them the money, fifteen thousand dollars, a fortune in those days, and left, despising his family, blaming them for Rosie dying. He said he didn't want his son to be adopted out, he couldn't bear the thought of other folks having what he was denied. He always planned to get back to Boston. Always planned on making back the money and returning it to his pa's bank.

Irish felt as if he'd been kicked in the stomach. All those years he spent wondering what was so wrong with him, aching with fear, unadoptable only because his father had provided the money for his upkeep. He almost laughed, the sound turned into a buried sob.

"What kind of a man was Drew Parson? Why was he in prison?"

"He stepped between a man and a woman who were having a fight outside a bar in Albany, Georgia. There were some old dilapidated rails. When Drew threw the man down he was impaled on an upturned spike. The man happened to be the son of a local judge, so they got Drew for manslaughter." Christian gazed down at his hands, his pipe long forgotten and full of dead ashes. "Drew was a rare good man," he said in his gravelly voice.

A rare good man. Irish knew he would carry that thought with him to his grave. There came over him a warmth, almost a living presence as if he held the spirit that was his father in his soul, and there seemed to be tremendous pressure behind his eyes.

For a long moment no one moved, no one spoke, and the silence was so deep the twittering birds might have had the mountain to themselves.

Awkwardly Christian began pulling his crutches beneath his arms, preparing to lift himself to his feet. "This was my mission all along," he said. "I never reckoned it would just be the telling of a tale." Desperation of a life lived unfulfilled caught at him. "It won't make up for everything—"

Irish reached out and took the gnarled old hands in his. "You've given me something for which I've longed my entire life. I've been wishing for my father, for my roots since I was seven...."

Christian blinked. "Mayhap it'll count against my sins." As he stared at Irish a small grin began to play around his lips. "You sure are the spittin' image of Drew. Gave me a start, you did, that first time I saw you." He twisted his old hand in Irish's and shook it hard. "I'm pleased you'll be on Talking Rock. And you can have electricity up to your place if you want."

"Thanks, but we've already got that worked out."

"Funny, isn't it," Christian mused, feeling as if a great burden had been lifted from his shoulders, "that the only thing that rises up from ashes is our past... just hangs there, lurking out of sight. I'm sorry about your pa. If I could trade places with him, I would. If I could bring him back to life, I'd do that too."

Irish rose to his feet as Jebediah ambled up. "You've given me a small piece of my heritage. It's a gift I'll treasure."

"Ya'll ready to go?" Jebediah asked, touching Calico on her shoulder. "I'm taking Christian down to my place. After we've rested up some we're going into Atlanta. Jerry Bass told us about a place that'll make him a shoe to fit that foot so he can get around without having to use anything more than a cane."

After the two old men had moved out of earshot, Calico turned to Irish. She could sense that there was something gnawing at him, some thought that he just couldn't absorb, a dull but driving rhythm. She wanted to find exactly the right words to say to him, but only the most simple flowed. "Well, no more notes," she said.

"No, no more notes," he repeated, and continued just to stand there as the fire died down and the wind picked up. Calico began to throw wet straw on the fire, smothering it. She knew with a certainty that it wasn't the time to try to explain about Judalon, that it wasn't the time to press him about loving her.

"I still want that bath," she said in a small voice for something more to say, reflecting that even if he did want her, there was still the specter of Belle who kept him a married man. "I'm going to the house now. Are you coming?"

He nodded but said nothing, seeming only now to realize they were the last remaining on the rocky slope. Calico pulled the blanket around her, closing out the slice of wind that lifted it flapping, and led the way down and across the river. Irish followed behind, his eyes on the ground, unseeing, stumbling now and again as did Calico in her exhausted state.

The answer came upon him with cataclysmic clarity. *Drew Parsons*. His father. "Calico!" he moaned as his knees buckled, every nerve ending he owned feeling as if it had been touched with a hot poker, and he began to collapse.

She spun around, grabbing for him, his weight carrying her down too. "What's wrong? Are you hurt? Why didn't you say something?" He was on top of her, pressing all the air out of her lungs.

"Wrong?" he began to laugh and she feared he'd gone mad. He wouldn't be the first the old mines had gotten to. "No, everything is right. Don't you understand. I know my family—not just my own father, but my entire family! I've known them since I was married to Belle."

He *was* mad. "What do you mean" she asked, pushing a little on his chest to keep from being ground into the gravel beneath her.

"Drew Parsons is—was—my father. He and Amos Parsons, my father-in-law, were cousins, sons of brothers. It was my father's place that Amos took over at the family bank. He might not have understood the scope of the scandal when he entered the bank, but after he took over, after he had total control of all the family trusts, he must have tried to find my father. May even have found him, for all I know. But I believe now that Amos somehow discovered that I was Drew Parson's son, and was therefore entitled to a share in the family fortune. Amos has probably been dipping into that trust since my father died...." His brain was laid bare. It was in his every gesture as he unraveled the mystery of his birth. "And even if he hasn't, this is one scandal that old Amos won't want. Don't you see? That's why he didn't want Belle to divorce me—so he could keep an eye on me."

"No, I don't see," Calico said with what little air remained to her. "And I can't breathe either. Will you get off me?"

He rose to his feet, pulling her to him, embracing her tightly. "I don't think it matters much that I'm married to my own second cousin. What does matter is that I can file a legitimate claim now to my father's estate. I'll trade my claim to it for my divorce to Belle."

"Good for you," she said, aloof to the point of scorn because his being free meant nothing unless he was willing to take seconds.

They were at the cabin, and Calico pushed forward, emerging into its familiar warmth with Irish at her heels.

"Slow down," he urged. "What's the matter with you."

"I'm worn out, that's all."

He grabbed her shoulder, spinning her about. "Look at me. I'm tired, too. Aren't you happy for me? For us?"

"For you I am." She relented some, because she *was* happy for him. Her silvery eyes were huge and gray and liquid in her face. "I—I'm not the woman you think I am. I don't want to talk about it." She jerked free of him and began to arrange her bath things. He watched her in tense coiled silence, searching her face for clues, until finally comprehension dawned on him.

"I'm going to make that phone call, but I'll be back, then we'll talk."

"Do we have anything to say to one another?" she asked, turning to face him.

"Yes, I think we do. I know we do."

Calico felt a sudden surge of restlessness and the

cabin began to seem small, much too small. She
waved a hand toward Irish as if to ward him off and
bolted out the front door. She needed to visit the scree
to talk with her mother.

Lowering herself on the old stump, she told her
mother all that had transpired. Pine straw was thick
beneath her feet, a carpet of dead brown needles that
in the spring would be pushed aside in the deepest of
night as tiny Indian Pipe plants thrust their delicate
stems into the dark, dying if a single ray of sunlight
snagged them. Death's flowers. But she did't want to
think of death now, only beginnings. Out the corner
of her eye she saw Irish disappearing into the forest
on the path to his laboratory. "That's him," she said
to her mother softly. There wasn't an answer, but as
the sun rose higher and cast its golden shadow, her
restlessness evaporated, and some minutes later she
went into the cabin, took her bath and lay down on
her feather bed to sleep.

19

THE NIGHTMARE WAS EERIE. Her father was calling to her in a troubled voice, and the river kept rising and rushing past her until she was drenched and there was Irish surrounded by fluttering bits of paper, a mountain of them and the river pulled at him, sucking him under, and she couldn't reach him because Judalon was holding her back and she wanted Irish but couldn't break Judalon's grasp. She called for help and there were her grampa and Jeb and Winnie and Jobeth standing on the scree waving tiny white crosses, doing nothing to help her and the mountain was talking, calling her to its subterranean bosom. She flailed her arms toward God, but the thin spirit wandered into the mists, and she knew she had to get away from Judalon else she would be carried into the mountain's depths and kept cold and empty for eternity. The nightmarish pictures kept coming and coming, never changing, so she struggled to open her eyes, letting flickering light dissolve the images on the moving mind frames.

And yet when her eyes were open, her feet still seemed thickly mired in the nightmare. She lifted her head to look at them and there was Irish, holding them on his lap, stroking them with his lean fingertips.

His gaze engulfed her. "I thought you were going to sleep until the end of time," he said, wearing a thin smile to cover his frown. She tugged her feet from his grasp, moving them back beneath the quilts. "I thought the same about you once. How long have you been here?''

"Since I got back yesterday. I spent the night on your sofa."

"Today is Saturday? I slept all Friday and Friday night, too?"

"Like a log." He was smiling.

She digested that information. "Is grampa home yet?"

"No. Winnie said he and Jeb are staying over in Atlanta until Tuesday. They forgot about this being a holiday weekend. I had Cups send my construction crew home early today." His eyes lingered on her, caressing. "It's just us on the mountain." She couldn't make herself hold his gaze.

"Do I smell coffee?" she asked.

"I'll get us some," he murmured, sensing she wanted a moment to herself.

The moment he disappeared Calico raised up, straightening her flannel gown, running her fingers through her long auburn hair, knowing it was in total disarray and worrying about how she appeared to him.

"You look more than good enough," he told her as he reentered her room, carrying two cups of steaming coffee.

"I couldn't possibly," she said, taking a cup from him, thinking she could get used to hearing him say it.

"You look beautiful when you sleep, too." He sat beside her on the bed so that he could watch her and felt her silvery eyes sucking him in. "I called my father-in-law...my soon to be *ex*-father-in-law, that is, from Jeb's. He's still in a state of shock." A low chuckle emanated from deep inside him. "Now I know what a novelist means when he talks about deep silence. Jobeth had a girl, by the way, and Judalon's in a cast from neck to ankle. He'll be laid up for a while.'' He was chattering away, and knew he should stop, but the expression on Calico's face sent a chill down his spine, reminding him of the cold he had suffered when he had been crawling down those erratic tunnels and fording slimy stratas of a black slough to reach her. ''As of now, you're going to have to give up going down mine shafts,'' he stated quietly. ''It's not something I want to think about my wife doing. I can't take it.''

''But it's how I sometimes make a living ... what did you say?'' She was bereft of air so that the question lay between them, little more than a cracked whisper.

''I said no more mines,'' he replied firmly. ''I'd never get any work done worrying about where you are or what you're doing or what's happening to you, if you're hurt or a mine's collapsed.''

It was now. Now was the time to tell him because if she didn't she never would, and then she would live out her life beside him full of fear that someday someone would say it. Besides, she had to know how much he knew or how much he'd guessed. She took a swallow of coffee, feeling it burn a path down to her stomach and took courage. ''When ... when we made love that first time, did you notice anything?'' She knew she was blushing, she couldn't help it. The question surprised him so that one dark eyebrow lifted in that cynical way had had of mocking her.

''I noticed everything.'' he answered after a second in a warm seductive voice that captured her in its velvet tones. ''I know every inch of you. You have a tiny mole just behind your ear, a thin scar on—''

''That's not what I mean.''

He sipped at his own coffee, guarding his mouth to hide a slight smile. ''I noticed that you're a bit oversexed.''

She had been holding her breath. She let it out,

making a sibilant hiss. "That's not what I meant either," she said annoyed.

"What do you mean."

Her nostrils flared. She would just have to say it outright. "Could you tell there had been another man?" There. It was out in the open. Her fingers clenched the cup she held until they were bloodless. If he wouldn't have her, now was the time for him to say. Now was the time for him to destroy her.

His grin faded into a grave expression. "I knew you weren't a virgin, if that's what you're driving at. I didn't expect you to be, although I found you, and still do, naive and innocent in some ways. On the other hand," he added with a smile, "you're a fast learner."

She leaned back against the headboard, needing terribly to brace her spine. "But you said...you *said* you didn't want any more seconds. You said you didn't want Belle because she was a woman any man could have. I'm a second."

He put down his coffee and knelt at the side of the bed, gathering her into his arms. "Calico, you've gotten things mixed up, and it's my fault. Maybe some of the customs you have up here are to blame, too." He buried his face in her hair, inhaling the scent of lilies. "I know what Judalon did to you. I know you didn't want it. I'm sorry you had to suffer something like that. If he wasn't such a pitiful bastard right now, I'd kill him myself with my bare hands for what he did." He wanted her closer, but there was the coffee cup she was still holding, her nightgown and quilts between them. He pulled away and she handed him the cup to set aside.

He caressed her face with his fingers. She placed her hands on top of his, holding them still so she could think clearly. "Irish, are you sure? Really sure?"

He slipped her gown from her shoulders, revealing

her softly thrusting breasts, the nipples swollen with want. He pressed his lips there—warm, moist, hungrily. "I want to wake up next to you every day of my life," he murmured, lifting his lips from her flesh with reluctance. "I want to die before you do, so that I won't have to face a moment alone or a night spent in agony with wanting you and not having you."

The sharp intimacy, the urgency in his lips, his tongue, which was doing wonderful things to her, made it difficult for Calico to continue. "But you did say you didn't want seconds."

He stopped then, lifting his head, meeting her eyes and seeing himself reflected in their silvery intensity. "Do you love me, by any chance? You haven't said."

"Yes, with all my heart and soul." She pulled his fingertips to her lips and kissed them gently.

"I have never in my life been truly loved. I think now that my father and my mother did love me, but my mother died, and my father was weak willed in some ways, though I think he was a good man in his heart." His voice dropped an octave. "Your loving me makes you a first, Calico. But," he added, his expression going strangely hard and dangerous, "if you ever look at another man the way you look at me, I'll shrivel, I'll die a slow death."

She looked up at him and smiled. "You're jealous. I could tell when Jerry Bass was here."

He gave a small laugh that was devoid of humor. "I'm not going to give up easily something I've craved my entire life." There was another craving upon him now and he moved her hand so that she would be aware of it.

It wasn't an offer Calico planned to refuse, yet she didn't encourage him. "I don't like you saying I'm oversexed and naive."

"Suppose I said that you were sexy, delicious and lovely, among other things?" he asked, getting up to remove his clothes. Calico watched as he threw them off, sending them flying in a dozen different directions. She hadn't noticed he was bad about that before. She'd be picking up after him the rest of her life, she thought happily.

He lay down beside her and she lifted her lips to the thick cords of his neck. He smelled so wonderful, all spicy, and soapy and clean. "You haven't said that you love me," she said, and her breath was wispy on his flesh. He trembled and Calico reveled in the new-found power she seemed to have over him.

"I love every part of you," he moaned softly, drawing his hands over her. "Especially this part...and this part...."

For a long while Calico stopped thinking, reveling only in their lovemaking—the way his hands touched her; the thrust of his body into hers making him a part of her, making them one; savoring his soft vows of endearment. There was in her a feeling of rarity, that she was experiencing something few others did, and she thought fleetingly of her grandmother and her mother. They too had been loved, and had loved in return. For a moment fright overwhelmed her that all this could be lost, that there would be no extension of herself into the future. "Irish...Irish..." she whispered. "I want children...I want a baby...."

"Tomorrow," he said, muffled against the slender column of her throat.

She gave a tiny laugh. "They're not something we can order from a catalog. Pay attention to me."

"I am."

"Stop what you're doing!"

"Stop?" he uttered with true incredulity.

"For just a moment," she pleaded.

He moaned softly, raising up on his elbows, looking down into her face, loving her, indulgent.

"Tell me that you want a baby with me," she said.

"I want a baby with you."

His hips, were beginning to move of their own accord, the mounting passion building between them, chasing away all words, all thoughts. But there was one more thing. "You haven't actually *asked* me to marry you," she told him, barely audible.

"I will," he murmured, his lips pressing warm and moist in the valley between her breasts.

"Now," she insisted huskily.

But it was a long while before the question was asked, lost amid murmured words of sensual love, and even longer still before an answer was forthcoming during the intimacy of flesh against flesh.

Outside the cabin the river flowed languidly, depositing golden grains in this trough or that. A gentle winter wind brushed the windows, and seeing the lovers entwined, went on its way, carrying with it the rumbling of the wild mountain and the murmuring of spirits, who seemed to nod approval as they gathered in the heavens to ride the stars from one galaxy to the next.